MAKE THE YULETIDE GAY 2
THE NOVEL

BY

ROB WILLIAMS

Copyright © 2018 by Rob Williams

Published by Guest House Books, a division of Guest House Films LLC.

All rights reserved. No reproduction, copy, or transmission in whole or in part of this publication is permitted without express written consent from the author.

This is a work of fiction. Names, characters, places, and incidents are either used fictitiously or are the product of the author's imagination. Any resemblance to actual persons, living or dead, events, business establishments, or locales is purely coincidental.

Cover Design by Robot House Creative

ISBN: 978-1987529661

www.GuestHouseBooks.com
www.GuestHouseFilms.com

Table of Contents

Table of Contents

Chapter	Page
Chapter 1	5
Chapter 2	10
Chapter 3	14
Chapter 4	20
Chapter 5	29
Chapter 6	36
Chapter 7	44
Chapter 8	52
Chapter 9	58
Chapter 10	65
Chapter 11	71
Chapter 12	77
Chapter 13	82
Chapter 14	98
Chapter 15	107
Chapter 16	113
Chapter 17	126
Chapter 18	144
Chapter 19	154
Chapter 20	168
Chapter 21	175
Chapter 22	180

Chapter 23	189
Chapter 24	191
Chapter 25	195
Chapter 26	201
Chapter 27	210
Chapter 28	214
About The Author	219

Chapter 1

December 18. One week until Christmas.

But for the lucky few to get invitations, it's also the culmination of nearly a decade of love, years of waiting and speculation, and months of planning.

It's the wedding of Olaf "Gunn" Gunnunderson and Nathan Stanford.

Early afternoon sun shines through the stained-glass windows of the small church, the colors dancing against the sanctuary's white walls and the elaborately decorated Christmas tree perched a few feet away from the pulpit.

Friends and family make their way between pews decorated with Christmas garland. In the center aisle, giant red poinsettias cap off the end of each pew, anxiously awaiting the wedding party.

In the back of the room, Gunn peeks his head out of the small room set aside for him and his best man. He knows it's the room usually reserved for the bride, but he's not going to let that bother him now. He looks adorable in his simple yet classic tuxedo. His light brown hair is on trend, as usual, but his forehead is wrinkled with worry.

"Ah, jeez! Look at all those people," Sven Gunnunderson bellows from behind his son, as he stares into the increasingly crowded sanctuary. "I'm glad I don't have to go up there."

"But you do, Dad. You're my best man," Gunn comments with a sense of concern. "Remember the rehearsal?"

Gunn turns to his father. For the first time in his life, Sven is wearing a perfectly fitted black suit and a white dress shirt. His tie, on the other hand, hangs limp and unknotted around his neck.

Sven lifts his head and scratches his beard, deep in thought. "I remember the rehearsal dinner."

"I don't want to talk about the rehearsal dinner. And get Mom to tie your tie."

"Oh, criminy," Sven says and promptly leaves the room in search of his wife.

Gunn stares into the foyer as more guests make their way to their seats. A large framed photograph shows Gunn and Nathan in the midst of a celebration, joyously kissing despite the tears making their way down their cheeks. Gunn smiles at the memory that the photograph brings, then his mind quickly skims over their two proposals – the first one, when Gunn proposed, and the second one, when Nathan proposed. Both were special, and both had led them here.

Gunn notices a closed door across the foyer and his smile disappears. He knows that Nathan is behind that door, getting ready for the wedding. Or, at least, he hopes he is. After everything that went wrong over the past week, Gunn is bracing himself for anything.

But he can never be braced for the sound of his mother's voice.

"Good golly, Olaf! Get yourself back in that room. It's bad luck for the groom to see the…" Anya flutters her hand in Gunn's direction, not sure exactly what to say, "…the other groom before the wedding."

Anya pushes Gunn back inside, closing the door behind her. She sighs as she looks at her son. "Baby boy!" she cries out, and then she starts. Again. It's been one of those days.

"Oh, Mom!" Gunn wraps his arms around his mother in a warm hug. Anya returns the embrace.

"But my baby boy is getting married!" she mutters into Gunn's shoulder.

"I hope so," Gunn whispers to himself.

Anya pulls herself away from the hug. She reaches into her ample bosom and pulls out a wad of tissue, which she uses to wipe her eyes and then her nose. And then it goes back into her bra.

Gunn looks at his mother, her short, round figure wrapped in a stunning green dress that makes her look even younger than her years. And to make the outfit complete, she wears her signature Christmas lights necklace.

For a long moment, they stare at each other as Anya continues to fight back her tears.

"I never thought this would happen," Anya finally declares, shaking her head. "I never thought this could happen."

"Luckily, the Supreme Court thought otherwise," Gunn replies, trying to avoid crying himself.

"You, both of you," she stammers, "you boys mean the world to me. You know that, right?"

"I know."

"After that Christmas dinner when you came out to us, I never imagined you and Nathan could get married. Legally! Ah, cripes, things change so much. Do you remember that Christmas? When we first met Nathan?"

Gunn laughs, his first genuine laugh of the day. "How could I forget? You tell that story to everyone."

"Well, I keep hoping some of Nathan's show business friends could make it into a movie, dontcha know!"

And there is it. Anya's giggle. The infectious giggle that can make anything seem better.

"So much has changed in our lives." Gunn eyes his mother warily. "Do you think you can handle any more change?"

"Well, I don't have any choice now, do I?" Anya replies. "But we're not going to think about that today. Today is all about you. And Nathan."

"And Dad needs you to fix his tie."

Anya rolls her eyes. "Of course, he does. I'll scoot and find him. And you..." She points a finger at Gunn. "You get ready to get married."

She exits the room, leaving Gunn on his own.

Gunn wanders over to the room's full-length mirror and stares at himself. He adjusts his cumberbund, his tie, his sleeves, his hair. Everything's perfect – except the look on his face.

"I can do this," he says to his reflection. "I can do this."

But as he thinks back over the past week and everything that happened, he couldn't help but wonder if he really could.

Chapter 2

December 12. It's the end of Finals Week, and it's hard to tell who's more ready for the semester break – the students or the professors.

In one imposing building, a professor stands from his desk and looks out of the window at the crowds of students enjoying the unusually warm weather in the Common Area below. An almost forgotten memory of his own time as a student creeps into his brain, then is quickly extinguished by a thousand other priorities, including the students finishing their final exam.

He checks his watch and writes "20 minutes" on the chalkboard. He adjusts his slim-fit maroon cardigan before taking his seat again.

In the front row, the handsome-and-he-knows-it Tyler Hopkins closes his blue book with a satisfied smile – but then, he has a satisfied smile about everything he does. He picks up his backpack, stands, walks to the professor's desk, and hands him the blue book.

"All done, Professor Gunnunderson," Tyler smirks.

But this isn't Professor Sven Gunnunderson. He's in the classroom down the hall. This is Professor Olaf Gunnunderson – known to his Philosophy Department colleagues as "Gunnunderson the Younger" or more often just "Younger," but better known to his friends as simply "Gunn." With his stylish haircut and perpetually youthful appearance, he looks barely older than his students.

Gunn looks up from his phone with a tired smile and takes the exam book.

"Thank you, Mr. Hopkins."

"I can't wait to see what you thought of my answers. I feel like I've learned so much from you."

Yeah, Tyler is that guy.

Gunn replies with a nod. "Thank you."

"Maybe there's more I can learn from you, Professor Gunnunderson," Tyler says quietly before leaning into close to Gunn's face. "Or perhaps there are things I can teach you."

Gunn stares at Tyler, not saying a word. His instinct is to chuckle at the boy's forward nature, but he would never do that. Instead, he reaches into the top drawer of his desk without ever breaking eye contact. He holds up a thick book that says "University Guidelines" across its black cover.

"I assume you're aware of the university's Zero Tolerance Policy toward sexual harassment," Gunn states with intensity.

"That's okay," Tyler says with a smile. "I don't mind."

"But I do, Mr. Hopkins," Gunn responds. "As would the head of the department – "

"You mean, your daddy?" Tyler interrupts, leaning heavily on the word "daddy."

Gunn raises an eyebrow. "I mean, the head of the Philosophy Department, the dean, and, oh yeah, my fiancé."

Tyler raises an eyebrow suggestively. "You're not married yet."

"And you're not expelled yet."

Gunn keeps his gaze firmly on Tyler. Finally, Tyler leans back. "I'm sorry for the misunderstanding."

Tyler leaves the classroom and Gunn shakes his head as he returns the University Guidelines book to his desk drawer.

It had been a long road for Gunn to end up back where he always swore he'd never go – the university where his father teaches. He never even considered going there for his undergraduate work. He didn't want other students or professors to think that he was there solely because of his father's influence, especially since he planned to major in his dad's field of expertise.

So off to a different college he went, where he met Nathan, and, well, everything happened.

Feeling a little lost after graduation, Gunn had chosen to spend a year in Spain as part of the Teach Abroad program. The experience had been incredibly rewarding, but being away from Nathan was too difficult, so Gunn returned to the states after a year. He stayed with Nathan in New York City for a month while he finalized plans to attend graduate school. Through the Teach Abroad program, Gunn had discovered his love of teaching, and he knew that he wanted to follow in his father's footsteps as a professor in philosophy.

But New York wasn't the place for him. He knew it, and Nathan knew it, but that didn't make the decision to continue having a long-distance relationship any easier. Nathan was establishing his career, and Gunn couldn't ask him to give that up.

Luckily, Gunn got into a grad school program in a little town in Connecticut, so he wasn't too far away. And as Nathan reminded him in their nightly Skype calls, "We're always together, no matter what."

Gunn is startled back to the present by a group of students turning in their exams. Gunn thanks them each by name and organizes the growing stack of blue books on the desk.

His interaction with the flirtatious Tyler Hopkins reminds Gunn of a professor he had in college. Someone who made quite an impression on his friends.

He grabs his phone and types out a text.

"Did Professor Van Devere RSVP for the wedding?"

Chapter 3

On the other side of the campus, in the Sociology Department building, Nathan pulls his cell phone from his pocket and checks Gunn's text.

With a smile, he types his response.

"Yes, Daniel is coming with Thomas."

"They're back together?" Gunn replies via text.

Nathan rolls his eyes as he replies. "For the last six months. Talk later."

Nathan slides his phone back into his pocket as he returns his attention to the students sitting in his classroom completing their final exam.

Nathan smiles as he thinks about his decade-long friendship with Thomas Krickstein. Thomas was the first person Gunn met when he arrived at college, but Nathan was the one who ended up having a closer friendship with Thomas after school ended.

When Gunn went to Spain for a year after graduation, Thomas became Nathan's rock for bouncing around ideas and especially for discussing his long-distance relationship with Gunn. Thomas moved to New York when Nathan was working at MTV, just when Gunn had moved to Spain to work with Teach Abroad, and the two young men shared a tiny apartment in the city while Thomas attended grad school at NYU.

With their dark hair and eyes, Nathan and Thomas were often mistaken for brothers, which they loved and often played along with, or for boyfriends, which they were always quick to shoot down. Never once did their relationship veer away from pure friendship. Whether that was due to Nathan's undying love for Gunn or due to Thomas's love of leather, it wasn't clear. But friends they were, and friends they had remained.

Nathan even stayed silent about Thomas's on-again/off-again relationship with their former professor, Daniel Van Devere. Daniel had been interested in Gunn when the boys were in college, but as he constantly ran into Thomas at the local leather bar, the two had started sleeping together. A couple of years later, they ran into each other in Manhattan, where Daniel had recently moved to teach at a small college in Brooklyn. Their relationship had resumed, and all these years later, they were currently on-again and coming to the wedding.

But Thomas wasn't going to be just a wedding guest. He had become so close to Nathan over the years that Nathan had asked Thomas for something special.

"A Jewish best man at a Christmas-themed wedding? Is that allowed?" Thomas had asked over the phone when Nathan called him to pop the best-man question.

"Um, wasn't Jesus Jewish?" Nathan had asked with a smirk, knowing it would set Thomas off.

"Jesus was a literary composite of several real men from that time period and a series of myths handed down from generation to generation, all written by men with their own agenda centuries after he supposedly lived," Thomas blurted out.

Nathan sighed. "But Christmas trees are so pretty."

That always stopped Thomas's argument. "You're not wrong there," he admitted.

That had been nearly six months ago when Nathan and Gunn had finally set the date after the Supreme Court's landmark decision in favor of marriage equality, a cause that had become Nathan's job for the previous two years.

After his post-graduation summer internship with MTV had turned into a full-time position, Nathan had remained based in New York, even if he didn't spend much time there. Between his production work on those mindless "Challenge" shows, which resulted in his traveling the country for months on end, and his trips to visit Gunn, he had become more of Thomas's houseguest than a roommate.

Weary of life on the road, and eager to do something more important with his time, Nathan picked up on one of Gunn's pet causes from his time at university – the fight for gay rights. Specifically, for marriage equality, which was the leading issue at the time.

His television production skills, his acting experience from college, and his vow not to marry Gunn until it was legal in all 50 states made Nathan into a determined and effective spokesperson for one of the many marriage-quality organizations based in New York at the time.

For two years, he spoke eloquently about the importance of the LGBT community gaining equal rights – not special rights, as the other side would argue – and he often spoke of his love for Gunn in a way that personalized the debate for television anchors and viewers alike.

On decision day, Nathan had flown Gunn to Manhattan to await the Supreme Court news. The couple waited in Nathan's office along with dozens of staff members and volunteers. They stood silently in anticipation, then cheered uproariously in victory when the decision came down.

The team's photographer snapped a picture of Gunn and Nathan kissing in the celebration, tears of joy streaming down their faces. The picture was picked up by the Associated Press and spread to news organizations around the world.

For many people, Nathan and Gunn became the face of marriage equality. And they couldn't have been more proud.

But that was months ago, and their 15 minutes of fame had passed, along with Nathan's job, which was fine with him. Nathan had grown tired of the travel, tired of being in the public eye, and most of all, tired of being away from Gunn. It was time for them to be in the same city, so Nathan gave up the Big Apple for the Arizona desert.

With Gunn firmly ensconced in the university's philosophy department – the same department where Sven Gunnunderson worked – Nathan at first had scoured the school's job boards, looking for anything to keep him occupied.

But nothing fell into place until a late-summer cocktail party for the university staff and spouses. Nathan and Gunn had immediately been recognized by one of the Sociology professors from their iconic photo. As fate would have it, a visiting professor had dropped out at the last minute, and Nathan was immediately offered a job (for the next academic year, at least) teaching a course on social activism in the 21st century.

It was a perfect fit for Nathan. The class was inspiring for him and his students, he could have lunch with his fiancé whenever he wanted, and best of all, they could plan their Christmas wedding together.

Now, with the wedding less than a week away, Nathan looks over a to-do checklist in a red binder as he waits for his students to finish their final exams. He didn't really need to do this, as their wedding planner had everything under control, but it gave him something to do.

Tuxedoes? Check.

Flowers? Check.

Catering? Check.

Wedding cake? Oh, for crying in the sink! Anya had "volunteered" to make the cake. Nathan smiled at the memory. "I'm gonna make that gosh darn cake if it's the last thing I do," were her exact words. Check.

RSVPs? He made a note to look into that when he got home. If he only knew who was going to show up without an invitation…

Chapter 4

With his briefcase filled with his class's completed exams, Gunn makes his way down the crowded hallway, recognizing the stressed-out looks on the students' faces. But then he sees a familiar face that doesn't look stressed at all.

Sitting at a desk inside an otherwise empty classroom at the end of the hall is Gunn's father, Sven. He leans back in his chair, mouth wide open, sound asleep. His eyeglasses dangle in the air, held on by the ever-present cord around his neck. His threadbare Christmas sweater is almost thin enough to see the psychedelic Grateful Dead T-shirt underneath.

A number of blue books rest haphazardly on top of the desk. Someone had written "Don't wake the professor!" on the chalkboard behind Sven's head.

Gunn rolls his eyes as he enters the classroom and assembles the blue books into a manageable pile. "Dad!" he exclaims. No response. Gunn gently shakes his dad's shoulder. Nothing.

With a sigh, Gunn walks to the chalkboard. "Sorry about this," he says in his father's direction. And then, he scratches his fingernails across the chalkboard, generating the most painful sound ever.

Sven jumps out of his chair, screaming. His longish hair flops in front of his eyes while his glasses twist around behind his neck. He looks around in shock. When he sees Gunn, he jumps again.

"Jeepers, son! What did you do?"

"Didn't you order a wake-up call?"

"Well, that's what your mother's for!"

Gunn thinks about that for a second. "Yeah, her voice does carry."

Sven shakes his head. "Oh, it's not her voice that wakes me up, dontcha know."

Gunn closes his eyes and winces. "I did not need to know that."

Sven slowly locates his glasses and puts them on. He looks at the desk in surprise. "The exams! They're done!" He picks up the stack and pretends to weigh it. "Feels like a lot of As."

"You should probably read them first."

"Fine," Sven reluctantly agrees. "Life was a lot easier before you were here to keep an eye on me."

Suddenly, a loud voice booms from the hallway. "Professor Gunnunderson!"

Sven and Gunn turn and answer in unison. "Yes?"

A lanky man in his 60s wearing a cliché tweed jacket with elbow patches steps into the room. "At ease, Elder," the man gestures at Sven, who shrugs and sits back down at his desk.

"What can I do for you, Dean Padial?" Gunn asks with hesitation.

"Don't be, um, scared, um, Younger," Joseph Padial, dean of the philosophy department, reassures him, with his trademark verbal starts and stops. Listening to his perpetually stoned father and Dean Padial have a discussion was one of Gunn's favorite sources of unintended entertainment. If the two men tried to decide where to go for lunch, it could turn into a half-hour back-and-forth of stammers and 50-yard stares.

"I, um, just wanted to say that, um, I'm sorry." Dean Padial stopped there.

Not sure what he meant, Gunn replies politely, "That's quite all right, sir."

Dean Padial nods for a moment, then resumes his thought. "Um, about your wedding. I, um, can't make it with, um, holiday travel and, um, all. But I truly, um, appreciate the invitation." The thought complete, the dean puts his hands behind his back with an air of satisfaction.

"Well, you will be missed, sir," Gunn says with sincerity. "And thank you for the present. We haven't opened it yet, but that was very nice of you."

Confusion crosses Sven's face. "Was I supposed to get you a present?"

Gunn scratches his head. "Well, you and Mom are paying for the wedding."

"We are?"

Gunn nods. "But if you want to get us anything else, I have my eye on a cute little Prius."

"A Prius, huh?" Sven thinks on that for a moment. "Is that some kind of sausage?"

"Very good for the environment. Good choice," Dean Padial pipes in.

"I try."

Dean Padial starts to leave, then turns back and hesitates a moment before saying, "I'm very, um, proud of you, Younger."

"Proud? Why?" Gunn asks with surprise.

"Well," the dean continues, "when I started teaching here, it was, um, a different time. I would have never had the …" he searches for the right word, "the courage to be as, um, open as you are."

Gunn starts to ask a question, but Dean Padial stops him with an outstretched arm. "I wish I had been able to bring my … my partner to events here on campus. I, um, couldn't even talk about him, really." He stops deep in thought. "I wish he was still here. He, um, he would have liked you."

"Thank you, sir. That means a lot."

Dean Padial holds out his hand, which Gunn takes in a warm handshake.

"Congratulations, Olaf. I, um, mean it."

And with that, the dean turns and leaves the classroom.

Gunn watches him walk away. "Wow. It's hard to believe how much things have changed in my lifetime. Or in your lifetime," he says to his father.

But Sven's only reaction is a started cry of "Dean Padial is gay?"

* * *

Gunn and Sven discuss their students and their remaining classes as they meander across the campus towards the faculty parking lot. They each had one more final to give – Sven finished up the next day with his senior honors seminar, and Gunn the day after that with his Introduction to Philosophy class.

"A Christmas wedding seemed like a good idea, but with all these exams to grade..." Gunn shook his head with exaggerated exhaustion.

"Take 'em on your honeymoon. It'll give you something to do," Sven responds as if that was the most logical answer in the world.

"As strange as it might sound, I kinda have other plans for my honeymoon," Gunn says, the implication weighing heavy in the air.

"Sightseeing?" Sven asks.

Gunn thinks about it. "Well, if you mean the pillows at our LGBTQBnB.com rental in Maui, then yes. Sightseeing."

Sven looks even more confused. "Why would you be looking at the pillows? Wouldn't they be behind your head?"

"Um…" Gunn thinks about it. "Sometimes."

And Sven thinks about that as he stares off into the distance. He finally comes back with an understanding look in his eyes. "Oh! Yeah, that's a good one, for sure. Hey, you know what your mom likes? You should try this. You take a pillow and put it underneath your –"

"Please stop, Dad," Gunn interrupts him. "Way too much information."

"Fine!" Sven relents. As they approach Gunn's car, they see Nathan waiting for them, leaning against the trunk.

"Hey, babe," Gunn greets Nathan with a quick kiss.

"Hey, Gunn. Sven." Nathan greets his future father-in-law with a nod. "What are my two favorite Gunnunderson men talking about?"

"I was telling Olaf here about how his mom likes it when I –"

"Dad!" Gunn yells out, trying to stop his father from revealing any more details.

Nathan giggles. At this point, he's used to Sven dropping information about his sex life with Anya without even realizing it. Between that and Anya also wanting to be open about her son's life, and of course, Anya's booming bedroom voice whenever the boys had stayed with them in the past, Nathan knew far more about them than he needed to.

"That reminds me," Sven adds out of nowhere, "I need to pick up some batteries on the way home."

"Batteries?" Gunn asks. "For... oh. Never mind."

"You boys good in that department?" Sven asks.

Gunn and Nathan stare at each other. Did he just ask that?

Finally, Nathan responds. "Yeah, Sven. We're good. We don't use a lot of batteries in our..."

"Nathan!" Gunn cries out in embarrassment.

"What? We don't."

Gunn leans in and whispers to Nathan. "But my dad doesn't need to know that. Or that we have anything that doesn't need batteries in the first place."

"Hey, if we can't talk about our toy chest with your father, who can we talk about it with?" Nathan says with a mischievous grin, batting his long eyelashes.

"Did you say something about toys?" Sven interjects.

Nathan stares at Sven, deadpanning, "Yep. Toys. Boys and their toys, right?"

"Little Olaf loved getting toys for Christmas when he was young," Sven declares.

"Oh, he still does," Nathan agrees, then turns to Gunn. "Remember when you were in Spain and I sent you –"

"Yep," Gunn says all too quickly. "I remember. No need to talk about it."

"What did you call it?" Nathan asks, trying not to laugh.

Gunn stares daggers at his fiancé. "It's not important."

Sven laughs. "He always liked to name his toys, even if they already had a name. Once we got him a stuffed elephant. Good golly, its trunk was this long!" He holds his hands about 10 inches apart. "What did you call that thing?"

Gunn clears his throat. "Kevin. His name was Kevin."

Nathan chuckles. "Kevin the elephant? Why?

"I don't remember."

"Oh, I do," Sven says. "You said he reminded you of that kid on your swim team."

"Oh, really?" Nathan asks with raised eyebrows.

Gunn sighs and shakes his head.

"Anyway," Sven directs his attention to Nathan, "if Olaf wants any toys for Christmas, you let me know and I'll take care of it. It's a father's job, you know."

Gunn leans in and kisses Nathan, only to keep him from responding. "Don't. You. Dare." Gunn stares deep into Nathan's eyes, trying to be serious, but he can't stop the grin on his lips.

"Sir, yes, sir!" Nathan says.

But before Gunn can say anything else, both his and Nathan's cell phones beep.

They look at their phones, then at each other.

"The wedding planner," they say in unison.

Chapter 5

"We only have a week to go and there's still so much to do and I need your full attention or else this will be as spectacular a failure as my third marriage and nobody wants that, do they?"

The wedding planner stops, waiting for a reply. When she doesn't get one, she loudly snaps her fingers in front of Gunn's and then Nathan's faces.

"Yoo hoo! Boys! Are you listening?"

The boys look up from their detailed binders at their wedding planner – Heather Mancuso.

Standing in front of Gunn and Nathan wearing a black sweatsuit with a leopard-print faux fur collar, Heather holds an even larger binder against her impressive cleavage. Post-It notes jump off the pages and fall to the floor with her every move.

"Yes, Mrs. Mancuso," they reply together.

"Good," Heather says, a wicked smile creeping onto her face. "I know men in general think weddings just come together without any work, but you! I thought the gays would know better!"

Before she can admonish them further, Heather's phone rings and she checks the screen.

"It's the soloist. Anything I should tell her? Any more changes or are we good?" Before they can answer, she repeats, "Are? We? Good?"

"Well…" Nathan stammers.

Heather rolls her eyes and answers the phone. "Hold on, Gloria."

Heather stares at Nathan. "Yes?"

"I was just wondering," Nathan says thoughtfully. "Could she sing *All The Single Ladies* during the ceremony?"

Gunn playfully slaps Nathan's arm. "No! We decided she was going to sing *The Shape of My Heart*!"

Nathan clutches his collar in mock despair. "You would choose the Boys over Beyoncé?"

Gunn pretends to think it over. "Well, three of them."

Heather turns, ignoring them, and moves into the dining room to take the phone call.

Gunn leans back on their brown leather sofa and puts his feet on the coffee table.

"We should really stop giving her such a hard time," Gunn says to Nathan.

"I know," Nathan responds as he curls up against Gunn's chest. "Let's wrap this up quickly so I can give you a hard time." He looks up at Gunn and wiggles his eyebrows seductively.

"Deal." Gunn seals the decision with a kiss.

As they lean back quietly and wait for Heather to return, Gunn looks around the house – no, the home – he has made with Nathan, and he smiles.

After years of living apart, he couldn't believe that they were finally in the same town, in the same house, and about to get married. A part of him had enjoyed the travel, enjoyed the literal and metaphorical education he received in so many different cities, and he definitely enjoyed, as his mom called it, their "oh so modern" relationship.

Sometimes, Gunn didn't know how they had made their long-distance relationship work for so long. But other times, like now, as he looked at Nathan cuddled up in his arms, he knew. It was true love. Always had been. Always would be.

He took a moment to admire their house – their first real house together. It wasn't an apartment. It wasn't shared with Thomas. It wasn't temporary. Okay, it was still a rental, but Gunn was already talking with the owner about the possibility of him and Nathan buying it and making it their home for real.

Pictures, artwork, and souvenirs from their varied travels decorate the sizeable living room, which is filled with furniture chosen for comfort as well as looks. The large, padded coffee table on which Gunn rests his feet complements the furniture without matching it (which was a much bigger deal to Nathan than to Gunn). The comfy sofa was nestled amongst an eclectic selection of tables and lamps, opposite a pair of tan club chairs, while a black Eames chair rested in the corner, angled toward the massive TV mounted on the wall.

And of course, on top of their usual furnishings is a layer of Christmas decorations, with a beautiful tree covered in tinsel, lights, and ornaments standing to the right of the TV. It's nowhere close to what his mom does for Christmas, but Gunn loves it, especially since everything had been picked out by Nathan and him together.

Through an archway stands the dining room, with its masculine wood table that could seat 12 if absolutely necessary, and an entire wall of built-in shelves that were stuffed with photos, mementos, trinkets, and of course, lots and lots of books. Where the dining table would normally hold a tasteful vase or an arrangement of fresh flowers, tonight it holds a stack of wedding presents – some in simple white or silver wrapping, others in bright Christmas wrapping. They had decided to wait until after the wedding to open the presents, and Gunn was using all of his willpower to avoid checking their wedding registries and seeing what items had been purchased.

Heather paces the room, still on the phone, her close-cropped blonde hair and statement jewelry illuminated by the vintage chandelier hanging over the dining table.

Nathan had commented many times in the past that these two rooms were bigger than the apartment he had shared with Thomas in New York, and that the dining room alone was nearly double the size of the couple's first dorm room. Add in the first-floor home office that was practically expected in a university town, the bigger-than-needed kitchen, the downstairs powder room, and then the two large bedrooms and en suite bathrooms upstairs, and Gunn had somehow ended up with a house bigger than the one his parents lived in.

But he didn't care if it meant coming home every night to Nathan.

Gunn kisses the top of Nathan's head as Heather hangs up her phone and comes back into the living room.

"Your singer, Gloria, is all set with the song..." She checks her notes. "*Fall Into Love*. I'm afraid I don't know that one."

"It's one of our favorites, but we decided to do something different instead," Gunn states.

"Something more traditional? *Ave Maria*, maybe?"

"Well, actually, yes," Nathan replies in surprise. "That's exactly what we selected. Did I not tell you that?"

"Um, no," Heather says, perturbed, as she makes notes in her binder. "Why are you having *Ave Maria* at your wedding? Did you convert to Catholicism when I wasn't looking?"

Gunn points at Nathan. "He thinks it's pretty."

"It is pretty. But besides that, we don't really do traditional, so I thought we'd shake things up and do something super traditional," Nathan replies. "The old double fake."

"We agreed on a church wedding," Gunn adds. "That's traditional, too."

"I'd still rather have it on a mini-golf course," Nathan pouts.

"A mini-golf course?" Heather repeats in disbelief. "Why on earth would you want to get married on a mini-golf course?"

Nathan and Gunn look at each other and then burst into laughter.

"Is this a gay thing that I don't get?" Heather asks suspiciously.

"Let's just say it is," Nathan nods.

Heather rolls her eyes and returns to the list. "We can use the singer I already have on the list, and I guess we can use the church organist for *Ave Maria*. Nathan, dear, when do your parents arrive?"

"The 15th."

"No, it's the 14th," Gunn corrects him.

"No, it's the 15th. I think." But Nathan doesn't sound sure.

"It's the 14th," Gunn says to Heather with conviction. "I remember because it's the day after my last final."

Nathan nods. "That's right. And their flight gets in early enough for us all to have dinner together, but not early enough that we have to spend all day with them."

"When was the last time you talked to them?" Gunn asks.

"My mom texted me yesterday. Haven't actually talked to my dad in awhile."

"Is everything okay?" Gunn asks, concerned.

"Yeah, it's fine," Nathan dismisses his concern with a wave of his arm. "I'll check with them tomorrow."

Heather waits for them to finish talking. And they finally notice that Heather is waiting for them to finish talking.

"Can we get back to work now?"

Gunn and Nathan look at each other, and with a sigh, then both sit up and grab their binders.

Chapter 6

Thousands of lights. Hundreds of ornaments. Dozens of Santas. Ten Christmas trees. One Anya Gunnunderson.

But Anya isn't as careful tonight as usual. She tosses a couple of wrapped (but empty) boxes under the main living room tree without arranging them in perfect order.

She pulls a tissue from the right sleeve of her elaborate Christmas sweater (complete with blinking lights on the woolen tree), wipes her eyes, then blows her nose before returning the tissue to her sleeve.

Then, she reaches into the left sleeve and pulls out a gingerbread man cookie. She bites off the head as she surveys the room.

Her normally perfect hair is all askew, and Anya constantly runs her hands over her head with anxiety. Whether she's trying to fix her hair or mess it up even more, it's not clear. She's only succeeding in the latter.

But the living room is a perfect winter wonderland, as always. The trees, the lights, the wooden "Ho Ho Ho Dontcha Know" sign on the mantel – little has changed in the Gunnunderson house decorations over the years. A few new additions make their way into the melee every Christmas, but tradition keeps Anya from making too many changes.

To anyone on the outside, the house looks perfect. But to Anya, there's something missing.

She plops down on the couch with exhaustion, nibbling on the cookie as she scans the room, looking for something out of place.

"For crying in the sink!" she declares to no one in particular. "What am I missing?" She pauses, and then starts crying quietly. "Besides my baby boyyyyyyyyyyyyyyy!" she wails.

From the kitchen, the sound of the basement door opening and closing echoes into the room. Sven enters the dining area of the large room, a cloud of smoke trailing behind him.

Anya angrily yells for him to stop. "You stay right there if you know what's good for you."

Sven pauses in the doorway, his mouth dramatically held closed.

"I don't want a trace of that smoke in my living room. Do you hear me?" She wags a finger in Sven's general direction.

His eyes bugging out, Sven takes a step backward into the kitchen. He opens his mouth and lets out a huge puff of smoke. "No problem, Anya," he coughs.

Anya sniffs the area. "Ah, jeez, Sven, it's all in that darn sweater. Take it off!"

Confused, Sven takes a sniff of the raggedy argyle sweater he's wearing. He doesn't smell a thing, but he knows better than to argue with his wife. He takes off the sweater and drops it on the kitchen floor.

Without looking over, Anya yells out, "You better not have dropped your sweater on the kitchen floor, either!"

"Creepy," Sven whispers to himself. He quietly leans down, picks up the sweater, and looks for someplace to put it. Finally, he opens the oven door and shoves it inside. He starts to walk back into the living room again, but Anya's voice stops him once more.

"If any piece of your clothing reeks of that stuff, you'd better take it right off, mister man!"

Anya sits in silence, gnawing on the gingerbread man. She can hear a few movements in the kitchen, but frankly, she doesn't care.

A moment later, Sven walks into the living room. Totally naked.

He sits next to Anya on the couch and picks up the newspaper from the coffee table. "Better?" he asks his wife.

Anya looks over at him, then looks up and down his naked body, then rolls her eyes. She is not in the mood for this. "Good gravy, Sven. You are gonna be the death of me."

Anya stands and walks – no, she marches – into the kitchen.

Sven watches her leave. Then he raises an arm and sniffs his armpit. Shakes his head. He looks down at his crotch, then leans down as far as he can and sniffs. He evaluates the smell, then shakes his head again.

"Oh, Mama. That's not the plant. That's just me!"

As Sven hears the sound of pots and pans being slammed onto the kitchen counter, the door bell rings.

"Come in!" Sven yells at the door.

The door opens and Heather walks in. She carries the wedding planner binder in one hand and a to-go coffee cup in the other. She glances over at naked Sven on the couch.

"Hello, Sven. Nice tan for this time of year. Is she...?"

Sven points. "In the kitchen."

"Thanks." Heather starts to leave, then takes a second look back at Sven. "I must remember to check on the mushroom caps for the reception."

Heather strides into the kitchen, where Anya has set out pots and mixing bowls and cookie sheets on the kitchen's large island. Anya searches furiously in the refrigerator, putting containers of milk, orange juice, and egg nog next to the sink.

"Can I help you with something, Anya, dear?" Heather asks, rather politely.

"I can find it," comes the muffled reply from within the refrigerator.

"If I can help..."

"I said, I can find it!" Anya's voice rises in intensity.

"Well!" Heather exclaims to herself as she sets the wedding binder on the kitchen island. She tries another tactic. "You know your husband's naked in the other room?"

"Yep!" is Anya's reply.

"And I saw him naked," Heather turns up the snark.

"Who hasn't?"

"Maybe I should go keep him company."

"Better you than me!" Anya yells as she finally emerges from the refrigerator. She holds a can of spray cheese, and with one quick motion, shoots a load in her mouth.

"Mmmmmmmmm," Anya moans. "Better. So much better."

"Is it that time of the month, Anya?" Heather asks.

Anya shoots daggers in Heather's direction. "I'm sure you don't remember what it's like, having hit menopause in the 80s."

Heather smiles. "Now, there's the Anya I know." She leans in and gives Anya a quick kiss on each cheek.

"How are you, dear?"

"I've been freakin' better, dontcha know."

Heather puts an arm around Anya's shoulder with genuine concern. "What's going on? Can I help?"

Anya takes a deep breath and spies the binder. "Did you need to talk about the wedding?"

"I did, but if there's something bothering you, we can talk about it."

Anya pulls the tissue out of her sleeve again and blows her nose.

"Can we just bake some cookies for awhile?" Anya asks quietly.

Heather nods. "Sugar or gingerbread?"

"Snickerdoodle."

Heather's eyes go wide. "Oh! This is serious!"

And the women get down to baking.

Anya glances at Heather and thinks to herself how far they have come as friends in the past years.

While Olaf was growing up and becoming friends with Heather's daughter, Abby, Anya and Heather had maintained a respectful distance from one another. "Respectful" meaning that they sniped at each other every chance they got. Anya viewed Heather as a loose woman with easy virtues – in other words, the neighborhood slut. And Heather thought Anya was a goody-goody busybody with no fashion sense.

Only after that fateful weekend when Olaf had come out over Christmas dinner (and Abby had revealed her true, saucy nature) did Anya realize how much Heather had been hurting in the years since her husband died of cancer and how her behavior had been her way of coping with the loss. Over slices of homemade pumpkin pie and numerous cups of coffee, that eventually gave way to a couple of bottles of Merlot, Anya and Heather became fast friends.

Shortly after Olaf and Nathan graduated from college and Abby had moved out of town, Heather noticed that Anya was feeling down and a little lost (or maybe Heather was feeling the same way). So she proposed combining their friendship with their mutual love of cooking – and the Home Groan Catering Company was born.

The company's success surprised both of the women, but they kept the business small, just the two of them baking in their home kitchens. Neither had the desire to really grow the business or take on a storefront or even hire more employees (that was reserved solely for serving at events). But they did occasionally take on bigger-picture event planning, including small weddings.

So when Olaf and Nathan got engaged and set the date for a Christmas wedding in their hometown, Heather had volunteered to serve as the wedding planner at no cost. Her only rule was that Anya serve only as Mother of Groom #1 and let Heather take care of wedding plans. And so far, everything had run smoothly.

But tonight, Heather watches Anya with a careful eye. She hasn't seen Anya become truly sad about the wedding before, and she wonders if there's more to it.

Anya keeps her head down and focuses on the cookies. She doesn't want to tell Heather what's upsetting her. Not yet.

"Turn the oven on to 375, why dontcha?" Anya asks of Heather, who does as she is asked.

A moment later, Sven tiptoes into the kitchen. He opens the oven, reaches inside, pulls out his sweater, and then tiptoes back into the living room.

Heather and Anya stop what they're doing and watch Sven's actions without saying a word.

Heather finally breaks the silence. "Your husband is an odd, odd man."

Anya narrows her eyes and takes another hit of spray cheese.

Chapter 7

"Who are all of those presents from?" Nathan calls out to Gunn from the comfort of their queen-sized bed. He leans back on a stack of pillows, his arms behind his head, his bare chest and stomach exposed by the sheets riding low on his waist. "I was too exhausted to check the cards."

Gunn calls out from the adjoining bathroom. "The new ones? Susan from my department. Grace from your department. Someone in New York, must be a friend of yours. And those two guys who met on your Extreme Jump Rope show."

"It was the Ultimate Tug of War Competition, thank you very much."

"Whatever. Two guys pulling on long phallic symbols, and everyone's surprised when they fall in love."

The bathroom light flicks off, and Gunn walks naked from the bathroom to join Nathan in bed.

Nathan watches Gunn every step of the way. He's always been turned on by Gunn's body, and more than a decade together hasn't changed that. He loves how much more confident Gunn is now compared to when they first met back in college. At the time, Gunn had pretended to be super confident, but Nathan saw through his bravado and recognized the shy kid underneath.

And as far as Nathan was concerned, Gunn's body had only improved with age. Since he had taken the full-time teaching job, Gunn had also been working out regularly at the university's amazing gym, and it showed.

Nathan stares at Gunn's smooth, muscular chest, and admires how it tapers down to a small waist. His legs have grown increasingly strong since they began their weekly hikes in the nearby mountains.

As for Gunn's ass, well, Nathan had no complaints. He reaches under the covers and caresses it with his left hand, while his right hand plays with Gunn's tousled hair.

"Mmmmmmm," Gunn moans playfully. "Why, hello there, Mr. Stanford-Gunnunderson to be."

Nathan kisses Gunn gently and whispers, "We are not hyphenating our last names."

Gunn runs a finger along Nathan's jawline and kisses him back. "We could combine them."

Nathan bites Gunn's earlobe. "Stanunderson?"

Gunn kisses Nathan's neck. "Gunnford?"

They both stop and look at each other. Nathan finally nods. "Yeah, we need to stop talking about this."

He lunges in and kisses Gunn passionately. Gunn responds by rolling over on top of Nathan. He pulls away and stares down at his fiancé.

Gunn notices how Nathan has filled out since college, but in a good way. He's added on at least 15 pounds of pure muscle, turning his small, wiry frame into something more solid, somehow more mature.

The small patch of chest hair that Nathan had when they first met had expanded over the years, giving him a nice hairy chest and stomach (although Nathan kept everything neatly trimmed, from his neck down to his nether regions). Gunn admires how Nathan's naturally dark skin had taken on even more of a tan since he had moved to Arizona to be with Gunn. He even likes the tanline created by Nathan's addiction to tiny Andrew Christian swimwear.

Nathan catches Gunn looking at his body. "What are you doing?" he asks, knowing exactly what Gunn is doing.

"I am admiring the man I'm doing to marry in a week," Gunn replies.

"Good answer." Nathan leans up and kisses Gunn before suddenly pulling away. "But..."

"But what?" Gunn asks, breathing heavy.

Nathan licks his lips. "I think we should abstain from now until the wedding. I read that it helps, like, revirginize you, or something."

Gunn looks panicked. "You're not serious? Are you?"

Nathan nods his head, then grins, and shakes his head no. Gunn lets out a huge sigh of relief.

Nathan playfully adds, "Besides, you are way past the point of revirginization."

"That's not even a word," Gunn laughs.

"Whatever. You know what I mean."

"Yeah, I do."

"Good," Nathan says, dead serious. "Now, shut up so I can…"

Before he can finish his thought, Gunn's cell phone rings and vibrates on his night stand.

"Do not answer that, Gunn," Nathan demands.

Gunn leans over and checks the Caller ID. "It's Abby!"

"Oh!" Nathan's tone changes. "Then definitely answer it!"

Gunn grabs his phone, and the two men sit close together in their bed as Gunn holds the phone out in front of them and turns on the FaceTime.

Abby's pretty face fills the screen. Well, it's mostly her wild hair, but she's in there somewhere.

"Hey, Abby!" the guys say in unison.

"What up, bitches?" Abby screams in delight. It's her traditional greeting to them. Her eyes then bug out in mock outrage. "O.M.G. You guys are totally naked! Did I interrupt something?"

And once again, the guys answer and nod in unison. "Yes!"

Abby laughs. "Then unlike Nathan there, I'll keep it short."

Gunn and Nathan look at each other, then both shrug. "She's got a point there," Gunn says.

"Yeah, so do I," Nathan replies.

"Ooh, gross!" Abby cries out, then returns to her normal voice. "But for reals, bad news. Doesn't look like I can get there until the day before the wedding."

Gunn looks genuinely sad. "Are you gonna make it in time for the rehearsal dinner?"

"When is it?"

Gunn raises an eyebrow in thought. "I dunno. Dinner time?"

"Ignore him, Abby," Nathan interjects. "Rehearsal is at the church at six. The rehearsal dinner is at 7:30 at a restaurant over on University Drive."

"It's next to that place that used to be a donut and ice cream shop when we were in high school," Gunn adds.

"The stoner hangout!" Abby screams in recognition. "So the restaurant must be where that vintage video game arcade thing was."

"That's it," Gunn nods in approval at Abby's recollection.

"Do you guys always give directions based on where things used to be?" Nathan asks playfully. "That's a sign of getting old."

"Uh, no. Getting married is a sign of getting old," states Abby.

"It's a sign of becoming an adult," corrects Gunn.

Abby rolls her eyes. "Whatev. And yes, I'll be there for the rehearsal dinner. I have a killer dress for it."

"Awesome," Gunn says. He pauses a moment, then asks with some trepidation. "So, any news on that other thing?"

"What other thing?" Abby looks confused.

"Abby!" Gunn demands.

"Fine. But no. No news."

"When do you think…" Gunn lets the question hang in the air.

"Trust me. As soon as I know, you'll know," Abby declares. "Capiche?"

"Pa-quiche," Gunn responds. It's one of their standard expressions with each other.

"Nathan, dear?" Abby asks in a sing-song voice.

Nathan turns the phone more towards him.

"Yes, my love?"

"Have I given you the speech about how I've known Olaf since we were kids and how I'm happy that you're making an honest woman out of him…"

"Hey!" Gunn objects.

Abby ignores him and continues. "…but that if you hurt him once you get married that I'll have to track you down and hurt you back and that women know an infinite number of ways to exact revenge on a dirty-dog cheating man because we share ideas, instructions, and contacts on a women-only website called 'Oh, No, He Didn't!'?"

Nathan clears his throat. "Um, yes, actually. You have mentioned that once or twice."

Abby looks surprised. "Oh! Well. There you go." She sighs and her tone turns serious. "I miss you guys. I'm glad you answered. I needed to see your lovely faces tonight."

"We miss you, too, sweetie darling," Nathan says, waving at the phone.

"Give Emma and Mark kisses from us," Gunn says.

"Will do. Night, guys."

"Night, Abby."

Gunn hangs up the phone and tosses it on the night stand. "Do you think she's okay?"

"I don't know," Nathan replies. "Did she seem kinda sad?"

"That's what I thought," Gunn says. "What if... What if things didn't work out and she doesn't want to tell us?"

"No. She'd tell us."

They sit in silence for a moment. Finally, Gunn reaches over and lifts up the blankets, looking at Nathan's body.

"I guess that moment passed," Gunn says.

Nathan narrows his eyes. "Don't think you can get out of the assignment that easily, Mr. Gunnunderson."

Gunn turns on his side to face Nathan, pulling his naked body close to his own. "I'm sorry, Professor Stanford."

Nathan purses his lips. "Ooh. Professor Stanford. I like that."

Gunn runs a finger down Nathan's hairy chest. "I'm sorry for bothering you this late," Gunn whispers. "I mean, so long after office hours are over."

"Mr. Gunnunderson, are you aware of the university's guidelines on sexual harassment?"

Gunn leans in and kisses Nathan. "It's okay. I don't mind."

Chapter 8

The next morning passes uneventfully for Gunn and Nathan. They spend the time in their respective offices on campus, grading exams.

For Gunn, it's a nice, relaxing exercise. His exam questions were looking for very specific answers, and in his mind, the logic used in getting to those answers was very clear, very straight forward. Sadly, not all of his students got the message.

Gunn had always been a good student and he did very well on exams and standardized tests. Nevertheless, he had gotten used to more "radical" students telling him that his success was due solely to his position as a cisgender white male.

When he was offered his associate professor position, the university had received several letters of protest from the friends and colleagues of another candidate. The dean had dutifully informed Gunn of the letters but also reassured him that he received the offer based entirely on his merits. The fact that the other candidate had proposed a mandatory freshman course titled "It's Always The Man's Fault" hadn't persuaded the dean or the diverse group of faculty members who helped make the decision.

But Gunn took the issue seriously and treated every one of his students the same – good or bad. He shook his head as he read the essays by white male Tyler Hopkins, who clearly counted on his good looks and charm to make his way in the world, and he nodded in appreciation at the impressive explanations offered by Saundra Connors, a freshman African-American female student who Gunn tipped as the next great philosophic mind. He hoped to secure her time as his TA next year, which he knew would be a fight with the other professors, who would also vie for her academic contributions.

Gunn wrote a few more comments on Saundra's exceptional final exam before making a large red A on the cover. Gunn never graded on a curve, but he also never gave an A+ to anyone, with the belief that there's always room for improvement.

A rapid-fire "knock knock knock" on his closed office door gets his attention. He looks up but before he can say "Come in!" the door bursts open with the energy of the one-and-only Anya Gunnunderson.

Dressed head to toe in a garish (even for her) Christmas ensemble, Anya plops down in the chair opposite her son. "Your father!" she exclaims. "He's just…" She sighs heavily and pulls a wad of tissue from her sweater sleeve. "I don't know if I can… And your grandmother's coming! What am I gonna…" She throws her arms up in the air in exasperation. "That's it! Christmas is cancelled!"

As Anya blows her nose, Gunn stares at her, totally confused. "Come in, Mom. What's on your mind?"

"Hi, baby boy," Anya says wiping her nose. And then she starts crying – not for the first time today, from the looks of her face. "My baby boy!" she wails.

Gunn rushes over and puts his arms around his mother in a futile effort to comfort her. "Mom! What's wrong? Did something happen? Are you okay?"

Anya tries to collect herself, and she grows very quiet. She stares into Gunn's eyes. Then, her bottom lip starts to tremble, and tears pour from her eyes. "I'm fiiiiiiiiiiiiiiiiiiine," she cries.

Anya clutches her son close to her. Gunn pats her back and says things like, "It'll be okay. What can I do?" But Anya clearly just needs a good cry.

And that's when Sven's voice booms from the office door. "Ah, criminy, Mama! I could hear you all the way over in my office.

Anya's eyes narrow as she looks up and stares at her husband. "Your OFFICE is ACROSS the HALL!!!" she yells at him.

Sven's eyes go wide and he takes a step backward. "Oh, yeah, but it's a big hall, dontcha know!" He looks across the hall at his office door. "Very wide. Very, you know, empty."

"Yeah!" Anya agrees. "Like your head!"

"Okay! Mom, you stay here." Gunn stands and pushes his father into the hallway and closes the door behind them. "What did..." he starts to ask, then leads them both into Sven's office.

"What happened?" Gunn asks.

Sven sits in the large chair behind his incredibly messy desk, shrugging his shoulders. "I have no idea. She's been a little sensitive for a few days."

"Sensitive?"

"Testy."

"Testy?" Testy doesn't seem to cover what Gunn just saw of his other's behavior.

Sven sighs. "Fine. She's been a..." He hesitates, then whispers, "B-I-C-T-H."

Gunn tries to make sense of that. "You mean B-I-T-C-H."

Sven shakes a finger in Gunn's direction. "Don't use that kind of language about your mother, for crying in the sink. She's been a..." He whispers. "A bicth. It's a Scandinavian slang word we used growing up in Minnesota."

"Well? What does it mean?" Gunn asks.

"It's hard to describe."

"Try, Dad."

Sven stares off into space. "It's when a woman has been plowing in the field too long and the oxen can no longer distinguish her smell from their own so they stop obeying her commands and she's forced to turn her plow over to a younger woman in the tribe and focus her attention on less important matters like the schindedfraudeluskein."

Gunn sighs, confused. "The what?"

"The schindedfraudeluskein."

"What is the…" Gunn stops himself. "Never mind. Why weren't the men plowing the fields?"

"Oh, tradition, dontcha know. They spent their days doing something far more important."

"Like what?"

Sven looks at his son like that was the stupidest question in the history of questions. "Why, watching football!"

Gunn leans back against the doorframe in frustration. "That's fascinating, Dad, but can we get back to reality? Did Mom say anything to you?"

Sven rubs his beard, deep in thought. "Let's see. After Heather left last night, Anya said we needed to talk. So I waited for her in bed. You know, sometimes when she says, 'We need to talk,' she means something else."

"I don't need to know that, Dad. What did she say?"

"She started talking about her mom and sister coming, and my family, and the Stanfords, and the wedding, and…" Sven stopped.

"And what?"

Sven looks a little embarrassed. "And that's about when I feel asleep."

"Dad!"

"It's not healthy to stay awake when your body wants to sleep!"

"So you don't know what she wanted to talk about?"

"Who knows. It's like that time…"

"No, Dad. Focus. Mom is obviously really upset, and she's obviously upset with you, and I can't have her being upset five days before my wedding!" Gunn stops and corrects himself. "But this isn't about me. This is about her. Now, get in there and apologize."

Gunn points at his office door. Which is now wide open. He looks inside. His mom is gone. Gunn looks back at his father. "You need to find out what's wrong. You need to fix this." Gunn checks his watch. "And I need to meet Nathan for lunch."

Gunn goes into his office, grabs his briefcase, and locks the door. He looks into his dad's office. "Let me know what happens."

Sven nods and watches Gunn walk away. Sven's eyes narrow as he looks at the space where his son had been. "You bicth."

Chapter 9

Meanwhile, Nathan is about to deal with his own mother on a completely different issue.

"Hello, Mother," Nathan says, answering his cell phone as he walks across the campus toward the main cafeteria to meet Gunn for lunch.

"Hello, darling," replies Martha Stanford. "Did I catch you at a bad time?" And before Nathan even has a chance to answer, she continues her end of the conversation. "Now, don't be mad, but there's been a slight change in my travel plans."

That stops Nathan dead in his tracks. "You're not going on another Christmas cruise, are you?"

Martha laughs. "Oh, no, dear! That's not until next week. I leave the day after the wedding."

"You mean 'we,' don't you?" Nathan asks.

"You finally learned French!" Martha exclaims with joy.

Nathan shifts the phone to his other hand in an effort to not say something mean. "You said, 'I leave.' Don't you mean, 'We leave'?"

"Oh, that." Martha voices gets a tiny bit strained. "No, your father won't be going with me."

"What? Why?" Nathan asks, surprised.

"Like I said, a change of plans. Actually, and don't get mad, darling, but your father can't make it to the wedding."

Nathan freezes. He holds the phone away from his face and slowly counts to ten before resuming the conversation. "He can't make it, or he won't make it?"

"Can't, Nathan. Can't. He did want to be here but sometimes things happen that are simply out of our control."

Nathan looks truly disappointed. Mad, but mostly disappointed. "What is it? An important business lunch? Another trip to Italy?"

"I'd rather discuss it with you in person," Martha says in an effort to end the questioning.

"Fine. We can talk about it in two days."

"Yes, well, about that. I'm actually here."

"Here where?"

"At the hotel." Martha looks around the lush hotel lobby where she sits, her cell phone in one hand and an almost empty glass of white wine in the other. If she had been traveling all morning, you couldn't tell. Her loose white top looks impeccable while also setting off her stunning red hair and emerald necklace perfectly. At the end of her elegant white trousers are a stunning pair of red high heels. It's an elegant Christmas ensemble, and the waiter who brings her second glass of wine certainly notices.

"You're in town. At the hotel." Nathan states these as facts, not questions, in order to get his mind around them. "But your reservation…"

"Has been changed," Martha completes the sentence. "The lovely manager here, he's such a doll, he was able to get me into something today. I'm waiting for the keys now. So, how soon can you come over?"

Nathan grunts into the phone. "I'm in the middle of grading papers, Mother. And I have lunch plans. And..." Nathan didn't want to say that he had expected his parents two days from now and therefore thought that he had two more days to mentally prepare for their visit.

"And none of that is as important as seeing your mother. Is it?" Martha asks, draining her wine glass. "I'll see you in an hour."

Before Nathan can respond, his mother has hung up.

"Seriously?" he screams at the dead phone.

What could have possibly been so important that his father would have missed his wedding? That's something he would have expected from him years ago, back when he was still in college and not completely open to his parents about his relationship with Gunn. All that had changed over Christmas break his senior year, when he had surprised Gunn at his parents' home. Seeing Gunn come out to his parents had inspired Nathan to be more direct with his own parents, and to his surprise, they had responded positively.

While living in Manhattan, Nathan had visited his parents at their New Jersey home frequently. They had met

Gunn, and despite some initial problems, they had warmed up to him. "How could you not love Gunn?" he said often to his mother.

Eventually, Martha had given in. She didn't want to lose her son, and she could definitely see how much he and Gunn loved each other. She would never say so, but she was utterly disappointed when Nathan had announced his plans to leave New York and move to Arizona to be with Gunn.

Nathan's father had been a tougher nut to crack. Peter Stanford had always been standoffish with his son, especially after he learned that Nathan was gay, but like his wife, he wanted to maintain a relationship, and if that meant accepting his son's sexuality, then that's what he did.

The biggest positive surprise Nathan had ever received from his parents was when they had offered to pay for the wedding.

"I don't know how these things work with… with your people," Peter had said, "but I know we can afford to contribute more than the Gunnder…"

"Gunnundersons," Nathan had corrected him.

"Now, see, that doesn't sound right," his father had said.

All these years later, and Peter still couldn't say Gunn's last name properly. But that didn't stop him and Martha from offering to pay for the wedding. They even seemed genuinely disappointed when they learned that the Gunnundersons had already agreed to pay.

Nathan dials his father on his cell phone and waits as the call goes directly to voice mail. He starts to leave a message but a recording tells him that the mailbox is full.

On the drive from campus to the hotel, Nathan had filled Gunn in on his conversation with his mother. As they make their way through the hotel lobby to the elevators, Gunn takes Nathan's hand in his.

"Try not to be upset," Gunn says in a soothing voice. "Let your mother explain. I'm sure there's a good reason why he isn't here."

"Like homophobia?" Nathan says with disgust.

"Or maybe he broke both of his legs and can't travel because of doctor's orders," Gunn suggests.

"Let's hope," Nathan replies as he knocks on the door to room 403.

Martha opens the door with a flourish, her blouse billowing in the air as she moves. "Nathan, darling!" She gives him a kiss on both cheeks before moving to Gunn. "And my future son–in–law!" Gunn gets the two-cheeks-two-kisses treatment, as well. "Come in! Come in!"

Martha gestures for them to sit on the spacious room's oversized sofa. She turns to Gunn. "You must thank your mother for finding this charming hotel. The manager had to bump me up to a suite in order to get me in today, which of course, I couldn't turn down."

Gunn shrugs as he looks around the large suite. He notices the door leading to a separate bedroom, and wonders how much it costs per night. "I will tell her, Martha."

"Can we dispense with the pleasantries, Mom?" Nathan cries out in exasperation. "Where is Dad? Why can't he make it?

Before Martha can answer, a loud noise comes from the bedroom, as if a suitcase had been dropped onto the floor.

"Is someone in there?" Nathan asks before calling out towards the bedroom. "Dad, is that you?"

"It's not your father, Nathan. It's my assistant."

"Your...?" Nathan asks, confused.

"My assistant from the art gallery. I've told you about him, haven't I?

Nathan shakes his head.

"He started with me about a year ago," Martha explains as she refills her wine glass at the room's large wet bar. "Such a dear. And he didn't have anywhere to go for Christmas, so since your father isn't here, I suggested he join me."

Nathan pauses, mentally putting the pieces together. "Oh, my God. Is he going on the cruise with you after the wedding? Are you having an affair with him, Mother?"

Martha simply laughs. "Of course not, dear. Why, he's young enough to be... He's probably your age, darling." She calls out toward the bedroom. "Anthony, come out and meet the boys."

A handsome young man, indeed right around Nathan's age, steps out of the bedroom.

Nathan's jaw drops as he sees the man. His thick, dark hair that adds even more height to his six-foot-two-inch frame. His intense brown eyes peering out above a perfect Roman nose. His expensive slim-fit jeans and the skin-tight polo shirt that reveals his muscular chest and arms. But most of all, Nathan can't help but notice his mischievous smile.

"Hi, Nathan," he says at last.

Martha starts the introductions. "Nathan, this is…"

But Nathan interrupts her before she can finish.

"Tony Sambuco."

Chapter 10

"Hello, Nathan."

"Tony..." is all Nathan can manage to say.

Martha glances back and forth between her son and her assistant. "Do you two know each other?"

Tony answers her but never takes his gaze off Nathan. "We went to high school together."

Martha smacks her forehead in mock realization. "Oh, of course! You did mention that."

Gunn leans over to Nathan and speaks in a whisper. "Just so I'm clear, that's your high school boyfriend, Tony Sambuco?"

Nathan nods.

Gunn looks Tony up and down. He can't help but notice his intense good looks. He also can't help but notice that Nathan is noticing his intense good looks.

Gunn stands and moves to shake Tony's hand. His voice drops an entire octave as he introduces himself. "I'm Olaf Gunnunderson. Everyone calls me Gunn. I'm Nathan's fiancé. We're getting married. Nathan and I." Gunn releases Tony's hand and points to the ring on his left hand. "Legally married. Five days. Yep. Husband and husband. Me and him. Man, you're tall," Gunn concludes, looking up at Tony, who towers over him.

"It's nice to meet you, Gunn," Tony finally replies when Gunn pauses to take a breath. "You are a very lucky man."

Tony walks away from Gunn and toward Nathan. "It's really good to see you, Nathan."

"Yeah. You, too." Nathan holds out his right hand for a handshake. Tony chuckles at the gesture. "Stand up and give us a hug, for old time's sake."

Tony grabs Nathan's hand and pulls him to his feet, and in one smooth motion, embraces Nathan in a warm, close hug.

Nathan hesitates, then wraps his arms around Tony. Due to their height difference (Nathan topping out at five-six in the right shoes), Nathan's head rests against Tony's chest.

He closes his eyes as his mind races back to high school memories.

Tony being introduced to the sophomore home room on his first day after moving to town, and Nathan literally dropping his pen as the newcomer smiled at him.

Nathan and Tony bouncing lines off each other on the high school auditorium stage during a play rehearsal.

Nathan rooting for Tony at a basketball game while the lanky boy dribbles past three opponents to arrange a perfect lay-up as the crowd cheers.

Nathan sitting close to Tony as they watch a horror movie in Nathan's living room. They jump at the same time, then look at each other and start laughing. After the laughter dies down, their gaze lingers until Nathan leans in and kisses Tony. Their first kiss.

Nathan and Tony, naked, in bed, with Tony's face looking down intently at Nathan.

Tony stretched out naked in Nathan's bed, fast asleep, with Nathan curled up beside him, one hand resting on Tony's crotch.

Nathan's father throwing open the bedroom door to see the boys asleep and naked, before turning his back, calling out Nathan's name, and demanding that his "friend" leave at once.

Nathan waving at Tony in the school hallway, only to have Tony ignore him.

Nathan hugging Tony at their high school graduation.

That memory brings Nathan back to the present.

He pulls away from Tony's embrace. "It's been a long time," he says.

"It has," Tony agrees. "It was such a coincidence when I saw that your mother's gallery was hiring. Almost like a sign."

"Huh," is all Nathan can manage to say.

Gunn steps in and puts an arm around Nathan's shoulder. "Fiancé. Right here."

Tony smiles at him. "Yes. Congratulations to you both! I have a little present for you. I mean, it's not much, but when Martha asked me to join her on this trip, I knew I couldn't come empty handed." He leans in to speak quietly to Nathan. "I'm so sorry about your father."

"Thank you," Nathan says, before turning toward Martha. "Mother, I think we need to talk."

"Of course, dear, but could it wait until later? I'm suddenly so tired." Martha collapses onto a chair with a well-rehearsed dramatic flourish.

Nathan shoots her a look but maintains a plastic smile on his face. "I'd really like to talk now."

"And I'd really like to enjoy that little pink pill I took when we got here." Martha yawns. "Besides, you need to give Tony a ride."

Gunn pipes in. "I don't think Tony needs to be riding anyone right now."

Martha laughs at Gunn. "That's funny!" She looks at Nathan. "You never told me he could be funny, Nathan."

"I think I'm always kinda funny," Gunn says with a pout.

"Yes," Martha replies, her words getting increasingly slurred. "I know you do."

"Where are we supposed to take you?" Nathan asks of Tony, but Martha answers for him.

"Why, to your house, of course!"

"Excuse me?" Nathan and Gunn reply in unison.

But Martha's eyes are closed and her breathing is heavy. She's out.

Tony tries to explain. "The hotel is completely sold out. I certainly couldn't stay here in your mother's room. How would that look?"

Gunn starts to give him a snarky reply, but Nathan silences him with a glare.

"Anyway," Tony continues, "Martha said that you two had a guest room, and that I could stay there, which sounds like so much fun. We can catch up. It'll be like old times. You don't have anyone else staying there, do you?"

Nathan hesitates. "Well, not yet, but..."

Tony smiles. It really is a winning smile. "Perfect. I'll get my bag."

He disappears into the bedroom.

Gunn n alternates between shaking and nodding his head.

"So..." Gunn finally says.

"Yeah," Nathan replies.

"That's Tony Sambuco."

Nathan nods. "That is Tony Sambuco."

"Your first boyfriend."

"A long time ago, Gunn."

Gunn whispers in Nathan's ear. "You never mentioned he was so..."

Nathan anxiously awaits Gunn's next word.

"Hideous."

Nathan chuckles, relieved. "Didn't I?"

"No," Gunn says as he wraps his arms around Nathan. "He's like a troll. A tall troll. I'm amazed he can go out in public looking like that. Oh, and one more thing..." Gunn reaches out and wipes something off the corner of Nathan's mouth. "You're drooling."

Nathan playfully slaps him. "I am not."

"Good, because that Abercrombie & Fitch giant is apparently going to be sleeping 15 feet away from us tonight."

"You have nothing to worry about, Gunn," Nathan reassures him.

"Yeah. I know," Gunn answers cockily.

"Is this gonna be weird for you?" Nathan asks.

"Why? Is this gonna be weird for you?" Gunn asks right back.

"No! No, no, no," Nathan repeats.

Gunn nods his head. "So, pretty weird, huh?"

Nathan holds up his right hand, the thumb and index fingers less than an inch apart. "Little bit."

Inside the suite's bedroom door, Tony stands, listening, a devious smile on his face.

Chapter 11

"So what did he say?"

Gunn had waited as long as he could to interrogate Nathan about his day with his first boyfriend.

After they brought Tony to their house, Gunn had needed to return to campus to finish grading papers and to prepare for his last class the next day.

Martha had declined Nathan's dinner invitation, claiming travel exhaustion, and Anya had also said no to dinner, for reasons that she wouldn't share.

Gunn had spent the late afternoon and evening at his parents' house, trying to get his father to recall what it is that his mother had wanted to tell him. But trying to get Sven to recall anything these days was a fruitless endeavor. Anya had spent the evening in her bedroom, refusing to talk to Gunn or Sven. In the end, Gunn didn't do much more than keep his dad company, which he always enjoyed doing.

When Gunn arrives home later that night, Tony is already in bed in the guest room, and Nathan is in their bed grading the last of his final exams.

Gunn takes a long shower as he waits impatiently for Nathan to finish. At long last, Nathan takes off his reading glasses, closes the final blue book in the stack next to him, and declares himself, "Done."

Two seconds after that, Gunn starts in with the questions.

"So what did you two talk about?"

Nathan kind of shrugs. "Anything and everything, I guess. I told him what I've been up to since high school, and he did the same thing. We had a lot to catch up on."

"Is he single?" Gunn asks, not even trying to be subtle. "Is that why he's here? Does he want you back? Or – no! Is he sleeping with your mother? Is that why your father isn't coming?"

Nathan wrinkles his nose in disgust. "First of all – ooh! No, he's not sleeping with my mother. Why would you even think that?"

"They seemed pretty cozy in that hotel room. Maybe he's a gigolo. A hustler. A dirty, dirty whore." Gunn's eyes bug out with the suggestion.

"Hmmmm," Nathan lets the moment linger. "You know, strange thing, I did not ask him if he has sex for money. And you think prostitution should be legalized anyway."

"Do not throw my beliefs in my face when I'm trying to make a point!" Gunn declares. "I mean, look at him!" He notices Nathan's eyebrows rise at that comment. "I mean, don't look at him! He looks like he worked as a model while playing professional tennis."

"Ha! He did not play professional tennis," Nathan replies with satisfaction. But that's all he says.

"Oh, my goddess. He was a model?" Gunn whines.

"Only for a few years," Nathan replies. "While he was going to art school in Paris."

Gunn laughs the maniacal laugh of the insanely jealous. "Paris! You've always wanted to go to Paris. Maybe Tony can show you around. And can we talk about how huge he is?"

Nathan looks surprised. "What are you talking about? He's not fat."

"Not fat. Tall. He looks like, I don't know, that Shaquille Bryant guy next to you. What is he, like six-three? Six-four?"

"Nearly nine and a half, actually."

"Six-nine and a half? He is not six-nine and a half, and for crying in the sink, that's not what you meant, is it?"

Nathan smiles and shakes his head.

Gunn leans back against his pillow. "How am I supposed to compete against that?"

Nathan cuddles against Gunn's chest. "It's not a competition. He's an old crush. You're the man I'm going to marry."

"Even if I'm not a model?"

"You could be a model if you wanted to."

Gunn positively snorts at that one. "They made me be an elf in the faculty Christmas pageant."

"Oooohhh," Nathan purrs. "Elfs are hot."

"Elves," Gunn corrects him.

"Whatever," Nathan moans. "I mean, there's Legolas..." He tries to think of another elf and fails miserably. "And there's you."

As Nathan leans in to kiss Gunn, there's a knock on their bedroom door. The guys look at the door, then back at each other. They reposition themselves, sitting up in bed, before Nathan cries out, "Come in!"

The door swings open, revealing Tony, wearing only his jeans. He reaches up and hangs onto the top of the doorway, making his body look even longer and leaner than usual. His jeans are unbuttoned, the zipper pulled down maybe an inch, making it clear that he's not wearing anything underneath.

"I didn't wake you, did I?" Tony asks super casually.

"No," Nathan replies, also super casually.

Gunn suddenly raises an arm and puts it around Nathan's shoulder. "Still up."

Tony smiles at Gunn's gesture. "I just wanted to thank you, both of you, for letting me stay here. I hope it's not too much of an imposition with everything that's going on."

"Why? What's going on?" Gunn asks suspiciously.

Tony raises his eyebrows. "Your wedding?"

"Oh, right. That."

"It's no trouble," Nathan reassures him. "We're happy to have you here."

Tony blushes and looks down at the floor.

Gunn takes that opportunity to whisper to Nathan, "Happy?"

"Ssshhh," Nathan quiets him.

As Tony looks up, he takes his hands from the top of the doorway frame and shoves them into his jeans pockets, pushing them down even more. "If there's anything I can do while I'm here, anything at all…" He lets the suggestion linger in the air. "Don't hesitate to ask."

And with that, he exits, walking toward the guest room and leaving the master bedroom door open.

Gunn turns his head slowly to face Nathan. "'Don't hesitate to ask'? What did he mean by that?"

Nathan gulps, not sure what just happened. "Maybe he's offering to change the light bulb in the pantry? Something like that?"

"Yeah," Gunn laughs. "I think he wants to screw something in, but it's not a light bulb."

"Gunn!" Nathan exclaims, shocked.

Gunn looks at the open door. "Oh, and he conveniently left the door open."

Nathan gets out of their bed, naked as usual. "I'm sure he just forgot," he says as he walks to close the door. As soon as he gets there, Tony reappears, causing a startled Nathan to jump.

"I realized I forgot to close your door," Tony says, saccharine sweet.

"It's okay," Nathan responds awkwardly. "I got it."

Tony smiles at Nathan. "Good night, then." But before he goes, he takes a look at Nathan's body. "Nice tan," he says before he walks away.

Nathan closes the door and sees Gunn staring at him.

"I think you should lock the door," Gunn states.

Chapter 12

Gunn checks his watch as he monitors his last final exam of the semester. The class is almost over, yet every one of the students is still in their seats, writing feverishly in their blue books. He wasn't too surprised, since this introductory class tended to attract a wide range of students. In this group, Gunn counts only four, maybe five, kids who he thinks will continue taking philosophy courses in the future. Everyone else is there solely to fulfill one of their required credits.

The class is proving to be a good distraction from everything else in his life – the unexpected houseguest, his mother's angry outbursts, whatever was happening with Nathan's father, and of course, the basic stress of his upcoming wedding. Only four days to go.

Gunn pulls out his wedding binder and tries to focus on the to-do list.

There's the tuxedo fitting this afternoon with his father and Nathan. He makes a note to remind the store that Thomas will be coming in for his fitting later in the week.

Gunn is glad that he and Nathan had kept the wedding party to just one best man each. They had seen too many of their friends, gay and straight, have elaborate weddings with six, eight, even ten groomsmen or bridesmaids. They had agreed to keep everything simple, and so far, it had worked out well. Except for a few minor hiccups.

He opens up the seating chart, finds the head table, and crosses out Peter Stanford's name. He is dying to know why he is missing his only son's wedding, but he knows it's not his place to push for answers.

Looking at the round table and its 12 occupants – Nathan and him; Sven and Anya; Thomas and Daniel; Heather; Abby and her family, Emma and Mark; and Martha. Peter's absence left an opening – should he put Tony in his place?

"I'd like to put Tony in his place," Gunn whispers to himself. When he realizes he had spoken aloud, he looks up, but the students didn't seem to notice.

"Professor Gunnunderson?" a student in the front row asks. Gunn looks up and sees Veronica Gomez with her hand raised. He tries to remember if she had ever raised her hand or asked a question the entire semester, but he's coming up dry.

"Yes, Veronica? Is there a problem?"

Veronica smiles and looks around at the students beside and behind her. "We just wanted to say…"

"Congratulations!" the class shouts together before standing and launching into a round of applause.

Gunn blushes at the show of emotion.

"We're all so happy for you," Sally exclaims. "My moms said to tell you congratulations!"

"And my dads, too!" yells another student.

"You're an inspiration to me, Professor Gunnunderson," says Ian MacDougal, the one openly gay boy in the class.

Gunn starts to say something, but he's speechless. "Thank you" is all he can manage.

As the applause dies down, Sally reaches behind an empty desk and pulls out a large, flat box covered in red-and-green Christmas wrapping. "We wanted to give you a little something," Sally says, handing the box to Gunn. "I hope it's okay."

Gunn smiles. "I don't know if it's okay, and I don't care." The class laughs with him. "Thank you all. This is... This is beyond sweet."

"Open it!" someone shouts.

Gunn pretends to think about it before pronouncing. "Okay!" But before he can tear at the wrapping, he stops. "Has everyone finished their tests?"

The kids sigh and yell "Yes!" "Open it!"

Gunn sets the box on his desk and rips open the wrapping, then opens the box underneath.

He looks inside, reaches in, and pulls out a canvas. Gunn guesses it's 18 inches by 24 inches. As he turns it over to reveal the front, he sees something that really makes him smile.

The painting is of Gunn, standing at the chalkboard in front of the class. His right arm is outstretched as if calling on someone, and his left hand is on top of his head, while his face is smiling. He recognizes the pose, even if he's never seen it from the students' perspective.

"It's called 'Good Answer,'" Ian states, and the group laughs. Gunn says that a lot in class, and the painting perfectly captures that moment when he feels like someone has given, yes, a good answer.

"This is amazing," Gunn finally says. "Who...?" He glances carefully at the signature on the painting. Jason Hitchcock. Gunn looks up as the crowd parts to reveal Jason, a short African-American boy, who slowly holds up his hand. Gunn shakes his head in shock. Jason had been one of the best students in the class, in Gunn's opinion, but he was also extremely shy and almost scared to speak up in public.

Jason seems embarrassed at the applause he's getting but also a little proud.

"This was all Jason's idea," Sally explains. "He showed us a sketch..."

"And we all pitched in to buy the canvas and the paint," Ian adds.

"But Jason did all the work," Sally concludes.

Gunn looks at the artwork again, incredibly impressed by the painting itself and by the gesture.

"I had no idea you were an artist, Jason," Gunn says.

"I don't know about an artist, Professor Gunnunderson," Jason says quietly.

"I do," Gunn replies.

Jason smiles at the compliment. "Thank you. And I wanted to say..." He pauses and takes a deep breath before continuing. "I grew up being taught that..." He takes another breath. "I'm sorry. I was told that gay men were all bad, unhappy people, and that they shouldn't be teachers, and shouldn't be allowed to get married or any of that stuff. You have proven to me that I was taught wrong."

Gunn bites his bottom lip to hold back tears.

"This has been my favorite class this semester, and you are..." Jason pauses, then smiles, a big smile. "You're the best, Professor Gunnunderson. And you've given me the courage to say that my name is Jason Hitchcock, and I'm gay."

There's a pause while all the students look at each other. Then, suddenly, they all burst into applause again, this time directing it at Jason. "I knew it!" Ian yells.

Gunn claps along with everyone else, then looks again at the painting. He's seen photographs of himself, but he's never seen himself in a painting. The happiness on his painted face is contagious.

"If that's what I look like," Gunn thinks to himself, "I am in the right place."

Chapter 13

"Make it stop, for crying out loud!"

Anya stares at herself in a large three-way mirror that somehow creates far more than three of her in the reflections. She wears a beautiful, sparkly, floor-length dress in hunter green that makes her look like a million bucks.

Well, it would if the zipper in the back would close.

Anya stands in the fitting area of her favorite local dress shop, a seamstress tugging on the zipper while Heather sits nearby watching the process. Heather wears a snazzy, low-cut, black sequined dress with, of course, a faux leopard fur collar.

"But it fit perfectly two weeks ago!" Anya declares.

"I can make a few adjustments," the seamstress reassures her.

"But I don't want you to make adjustments," Anya cries out. "I want it to be perfect NOW!" And then she starts crying.

Heather pulls some tissue from a nearby box and rushes up to Anya. "Careful of the fabric, Anya." Heather then leans down and says to the seamstress, "She might be a little bloated. I think Aunt Flo is visiting."

The seamstress nods in understanding. "I'll get my things and be right back."

Anya can barely speak through her tears. "It's not Aunt Flo. I'm just faaaaaaaaaaaaaaaat!"

Heather grabs more tissues and holds it up to Anya's nose. "Blow," she demands, and Anya does. A little bit disgusted, Heather tosses the tissues into a trash can and returns to Anya's side. "Look at yourself," she demands as she turns Anya to face the three-way mirror once again.

Anya does as she's told. She looks at herself and starts wailing once again.

Heather turns on her stern voice. "I'm about to say something now that is, frankly, very hard for me to say. And if you repeat it to anyone, I will deny it. Do you understand?"

Anya nods as she wipes her eyes.

Heather puts her hands on Anya's shoulders and stares into the mirror with her.

"Anya Gunnunderson," Heather says forcefully, "you look beautiful."

That was not what Anya was expecting. "Really?" she asks quietly.

"Absolutely," Heather nods. "Now, I may have said one or two things about your wardrobe over the years..."

"Huh!" Anya snorts. "Ya think?"

Heather ignores that. "But the truth is that you know how to dress your body. You always have. And this dress..." She looks at Anya's reflection in the mirror. "Anya, when you walk down the aisle of the church, no one is going to be able to take their eyes off you."

Anya wipes her eyes again. "Really?"

Heather nods. "Absolutely. And you have an advantage that most mothers of the groom don't have."

"What's that?" Anya asks.

Heather leans in and whispers conspiratorially. "There's no bride to steal your thunder."

Finally, Anya laughs. "Jeez, you got a point there, dontcha know!"

Anya turns and surprises Heather by enveloping her in a big, warm hug. "Thank you, Heather."

"You're welcome, Anya," Heather says with a smile. "Besides..." She stands and looks at both of their reflections in the mirror. "We curvy gals have to stick together."

Anya raises an eyebrow. "At least I didn't have to pay for my curves."

Heather tilts her head and cups her ample breasts in her hands. "And they were worth every penny."

* * *

A few blocks away, in the fitting room of the local tuxedo shop, a sales clerk stands patiently by that store's own three-way mirror.

"Is everything okay in there?" he says in a gruff voice to three closed-off changing rooms.

Nathan's voice issues from one of them. "Gunn, are you ready?"

"Ready if you are," says Gunn's voice from the changing room next to Nathan's.

"On the count of three?" Nathan suggests.

"One... Two..." Gunn counts.

And on the count of three, Gunn and Nathan throw open their changing rooms' curtains, step out, look at each other, and smile.

They wear matching tuxedos – slim cut Hugo Boss with narrow lapels, crisp white shirts, and simple yet elegant black bow ties.

"Wow," Gunn says, staring at his fiancé. "You look amazing."

"So do you," Nathan says, a huge grin on his face. "You look like one of those little grooms on top of a wedding cake."

"Funny, that's exactly what I was going for," Gunn responds.

The sales clerk's deep voice interrupts them. "Can you step over to the mirror please?"

They obey him, with Nathan stepping in front of the three-way mirror first. The clerk straightens the jacket's shoulders and checks to make sure that everything fits perfectly, which it does.

"Do you have a boutonnière to match the bride's dress?" the clerk's voice booms in Nathan's ear.

"There's no bride," Nathan and Gunn immediately reply in unison. They've perfected the art of answering that question.

"No?" the sales clerk asks.

"We're the grooms," Nathan says, pointing to himself and Gunn.

The sales clerk looks at Nathan, then at Gunn. And then, he clasps his hands in front of himself. "Oh!" he says, his voice quickly going up two octaves. "No one told me. That's fabulous!"

And the sales clerk relaxes and becomes his naturally flamboyant self. "Okay, you," he points to Nathan and looks at his reflection. "You look a-may-zing! That jacket fits like butter. Now, take it off. Take it off!"

Nathan takes off his jacket, who hands it to the sales clerk, who hands it to Gunn. "Hold this, sweetie." Gunn can only smile to himself.

The clerk checks the waist of Nathan's pants. "Stunning." He looks at Nathan's ass. "Stunning! Those pants simply complement everything."

He repeats the process with Gunn, declaring his shirt, "Absolute perfection!" while not-so-subtly squeezing Gunn's biceps. "You are a lucky man," he says to Nathan.

"Don't I know it," Nathan responds.

When the clerk finally declares them done, Gunn yells at the remaining closed curtain, "Dad! What's taking you so long?"

From behind the curtain comes a loud snort that can only mean one thing – Sven had fallen asleep and had just woken up thanks to Gunn's voice.

"Who's there?" Sven calls out.

Gunn pulls the curtain aside to reveal Sven, sitting on the fitting room's chair, in an ill-fitting black suit. Gunn reaches out a hand to help his father to his feet, and maneuvers him to the mirror.

"This is your father?" the sales clerk asks of Gunn.

Gunn nods.

"So that would make you the father of the…?" The clerk lets the question hang in the air as he glances over at Gunn and licks his lips.

Sven looks confused. He points at Gunn. "Well, I'm his father, like you said."

The clerk purses his lips and starts to adjust Sven's suit. "Well, we certainly have our work cut out for us here, don't we?" The jacket is too tight. The pants are too loose. Luckily, the shirt is just right. The clerk makes notes on a pad, and uses chalk to make marks on the suit itself.

After measuring Sven's waist, he says, "I think we have a pair of pants that would fit oh-so-much better. Why don't you take these off and we'll have a go."

Sven shrugs, undoes his pants, takes them off, and hands them to the sales clerk. Unfortunately, as usual, he's not wearing any underwear.

"Oh, my!" the clerk declares.

"Dad!" Gunn yells.

Nathan just chuckles and turns his head.

The clerk takes one more look at Sven and says, "We'll just change this from a rental to a purchase then, shall we?"

* * *

"Ladies, can I get you a mimosa?"

Anya opens her eyes and looks up at Rainbow, the lovely spa attendant who had been assigned to take care of her, Heather, and Martha, who had offered to treat everyone to a facial and mani-pedi at the hotel's luxurious spa.

The trio of women sit side by side in padded pink chairs, each wearing plus white robes, as three Korean women work on their toenails.

Anya shakes her head. "No, thanks, Rainbow. I'm more of a beer gal myself, but it's too early in the day for me," she says, sipping on her mineral water.

Martha, somehow looking elegant while only wearing the spa robe, rolls her eyes at Anya's comment, finishes off the mimosa in her hand and gives it to Rainbow. "Keep them coming, dear. Heather?"

She looks over at Heather, who still has half a glass left in her current drink. "Oh, why not?" she says.

"Two more, please, Rainbow," Martha says dismissively. The attendant leaves them.

"This was such a great idea, Martha," Heather says. "We have been so busy with the wedding plans, and just between you and me, Anya has been a little bit stressed out this week."

"Um, I'm sitting right here!" Anya interjects, and they all laugh, although Martha's attention is focused more on looking for her next mimosa.

"When in doubt, pamper yourself. And it's the least I could do," Martha says, closing her eyes and leaning back in her chair.

Anya looks over at Heather and mouths, "The very least," which causes Heather to giggle.

"Martha, dear, I'm still a little confused as to why Peter couldn't make it." Leave it to Anya to come out and ask the direct question in the nicest way possible.

"I am as upset as anyone, believe me," Martha says with genuine regret. "There are some people he works with who…" She hesitates. "Let's just say they're more concerned with getting certain business dealings done before year end than they are with family matters like a wedding."

"You give me their address and I'll write them a letter and let them know how I feel about that," Anya declares. "Especially since those boys waited so long for it to become legal and everything."

"Is that why they waited this long?" Heather asks.

"Ayep," Anya replies. "You know, I was so excited when they first got engaged. I thought they'd have a little ceremony back in New York City, which isn't my favorite place in the world, but I would have dragged Sven's carcass over there if it meant being at little Olaf's wedding. But then they said that it wouldn't feel right having a ceremony that didn't mean anything, legally you know, and that they were gonna wait until everyone could get married. And that's what they did."

Rainbow interrupts them to deliver mimosas to Martha and Heather, and another mineral water to Anya.

"What did you mean, 'when they first got engaged'?" Martha asks, sipping her drink.

"Didn't Nathan tell you that story?"

Martha shakes her head. "I hate to admit how long it took us to embrace Nathan's... choices. I sometimes think about all the things we missed during those years." She sighs. "But I'm here now, at this... cute little hotel."

Anya and Heather share a look, knowing that this is the absolute nicest hotel in hotel.

"So, tell me," Martha asks, "when did the boys first get engaged?"

"Oh, this is a great story," Heather says.

"Well, it was right after little Olaf got back from spending that year in Spain," Anya starts. "Golly, we missed him so. Now, Nathan was living in New York at the time, a tiny little apartment in Heck's Kitchen. Olaf came back to the US of A and was staying with Nathan for a bit."

"I remember that," Martha says, surprising herself. "And that apartment! My shoe closet is bigger than that place!"

Anya stares at her for a moment before responding. "Well, all righty then. Now, while he was in Spain, Olaf had found these simple silver rings. Apparently, he bought them and carried them around for months before he saw Nathan in person again. But when they were finally together, there in New York, Olaf decided to do something really classy." She pauses and wrinkles her nose. "Well, he said classy. I think it's cheesy as all get out, but it was certainly romantic."

"What was it?" Martha asks, leaning in with interest.

"Apparently, they spent the day together, going to all sorts of places – the Empire State Building, Central Park, stuff like that – and they ended up walking across the Brooklyn Bridge at sunset."

"Brooklyn?" Martha says with a little too much disgust than she should have.

"And little Olaf stopped them, in the middle of the crowd, and got down on one knee, and proposed right there, with everyone watching."

Martha smiles, touched. "I'll admit, that is romantic."

"And everyone clapped, which I just think is the sweetest thing in the world," Anya concludes.

The three women lean back in their chairs, smiling.

"Christopher proposed to me at our favorite Italian restaurant," Heather reminisces. "It's been closed for years, but we used to go there on every one of our anniversaries. He got down on one knee, as well."

Martha sighs and sips her mimosa. "Peter proposed to me on a flight to Scotland. I was going to meet his parents for the first time, and he leaned over, right there in British Airways First Class, and asked me if I would be his bride." She looks at the huge diamond on her finger. "How could I say no to this?"

She notices the looks that Anya and Heather are giving her. "And I loved him, of course." She takes a deep breath. "Still do."

And now, Martha and Heather look at Anya, waiting for her proposal story. Anya glances back and forth at them and gives in.

"Sven asked me to marry him in the basement bathroom of my parents' house back in Kenosha, right after I took the home pregnancy test."

"Oh!" Martha exclaims. "That's..." She can't even finish the thought, so she finishes her drink instead.

"He didn't have a ring, so he took some rolling paper and tied it around my finger."

"That's so Sven," Heather says with a sigh.

Martha just looks confused. "What is rolling paper?"

* * *

On the other side of the spa, in the men's sauna, Gunn, Nathan, and Sven lean back and relax.

"This was nice of your mom, Nathan. I've never had a spa day before," Sven says lazily as he opens his towel and leans back against the room's cedar paneling.

Gunn and Nathan share a look, shaking their head at Sven's immense comfort with being totally naked.

"When in doubt, pamper yourself. That's her motto," Nathan replies. "It would have been a nice opportunity for you and my dad to get to know each other. But..." He leaves the fact of his father's absence unsaid.

Sven and Peter had, of course, met several times over the years, but they both realized that they had very little in common. Peter had come a long way in accepting his son, and Sven respected that, but their conversations tended to stay in areas with little chance for conflict. The weather and golf won out in the end.

"Maybe he'll still make it for the ceremony," Sven offers.

"I haven't even been able to get my mom to tell me what happened, and my dad isn't answering his phone," Nathan declares. "I doubt he'll show up."

"Well, if he doesn't, it's his loss," Sven adds.

Nathan smiles and looks at Sven. It seems appropriate that he's naked since he was naked (well, almost) when they first met. That Christmas break, senior year, Sven had opened his front door, his robe flowing open behind him, not knowing who Nathan was or why he was there. But Nathan knew how much he and Anya both loved him now. They had treated him better than his own parents ever had.

Nathan was not letting his anger with his father overcome his happiness about his wedding. Nor was he letting the sudden appearance of his high school boyfriend – or whatever his mother's motive for bringing him here – deter him from focusing on what was important.

He did have to admit that the couples massage that he and Gunn just had had been incredibly relaxing, just what they needed. Sven had apparently fallen asleep during his massage, which didn't surprise him, and hitting the sauna before they all got together for dinner seemed like a good idea.

Since they were the only three men in the sauna and since Sven was resting an arm over his eyes, Nathan scooted closer to Gunn and whispered in his ear. "Think you could get your dad to leave for a bit?" He puts a hand on Gunn's leg.

Gunn smirks at him. "You and your steam room fantasies."

"It's a sauna, not a steam room, and it hasn't always been just a fantasy. Remember?"

Gunn smiles. "I do."

"Get your dad to leave, and…"

Nathan whispers something in Gunn's ear. His eyes open wide. "Dad, isn't it time for you to… be somewhere else?"

Sven doesn't look up. "Nope. I'm good."

Gunn looks at Nathan and shrugs as if to say, "What am I gonna do?"

Nathan responds by opening up his towel and giving Gunn a peek underneath.

"There's munchies in the locker room," Gunn croaks out to his dad.

That gets Sven's attention. He looks up. "Munchies?"

"Bagels. Chips. Even bagel chips. All sorts of stuff. And it's free."

"I'm outta here," Sven says as he stands. But before he leaves, he turns to Gunn. "And where is the locker room again?"

"Make a right, past the showers, make a left, and there it is," Gunn directs him.

Sven's eyes move back in forth in thought. "My right or your right?"

Gunn takes a deep breath and looks at Nathan. "I'll be right back," he says before leading his father out of the sauna.

Nathan moves onto his back with a laugh, wiping the sweat off his face and chest. He closes his eyes as he waits for Gunn to return.

Soon, he hears the sauna door open. "Took you long enough," he says as he slowly removes his towel.

"That's a sight for sore eyes."

Nathan opens his eyes, realizing that that wasn't Gunn's voice.

He looks over and sees Tony standing there, a towel thrown over his shoulder where it doesn't cover up anything.

Nathan sits up and moves his towel over his crotch.

"Tony! What are you doing here?"

Tony saunters over – for there is no other way to describe his walk except as a saunter. "Your mom told me about the men's spa day. Thought I'd join you."

Tony sits down right next to Nathan, who can't help but look down before turning his head away.

"Just like the old days," Tony says.

"Except that I'm engaged," Nathan replies.

"Which means that you're not married yet," Tony counters. He inches his body closer to Nathan's. "You still have those steam room fantasies?"

Nathan gulps, hard. "This is a sauna."

"Whatever." And with that, Tony leans in and kisses Nathan.

Nathan pushes him away, scooting back. Only then does he see Gunn standing just inside the sauna door.

Tony follows Nathan's gaze and smiles when he, too, sees Gunn. Tony licks his lips. "I suppose I could give both of you your wedding present right here." He turns to Nathan. "This is just what we talked about back in high school." Then he looks back at Gunn. "What do you say?"

Chapter 14

To say that dinner that night is awkward would be a massive understatement.

Gunn and Nathan sit at opposite ends of the restaurant's long table, not really speaking to each other.

Sven sits next to Nathan, which causes Anya to sit next to Gunn, as far away from her husband as possible and close to Heather, who takes the other seat next to Gunn.

Martha and Tony take the center seats on either side of the table.

Tony glances back and forth from Gunn to Nathan, while Martha glances at the wine list.

"Is rosé good for everyone?" Martha asks to no one in particular. Not getting an answer, she turns to the waiter. "We'll take two bottles of the rosé." She looks at the extremely quiet table. "Better make it three."

The waiter rushes off and everyone stares intently at their menus.

Ever the good hostess, Martha notices the lone empty chair at the table for eight. "Are we missing someone?"

Everyone turns to the empty chair as if on cue, then Heather's laugh breaks the silence. "My bad. I was hoping a friend of mine could join us, but you know how the holidays can be."

Tony responds. "No. How can they be?"

Heather pauses, not sure how to answer that. "Busy," she says with a snarl.

"Is this friend of yours coming to the wedding?" Anya asks. "You've been sneaking off for a lot of secret meetings lately."

"Maybe. I don't know," Heather answers with measured enthusiasm.

Anya snaps a breadstick in half as she evaluates Heather. "What is it you're not telling me about this guy?"

Heather straightens the napkin in her lap. "I'm not not telling you anything, Anya, dear." She feels everyone's eyes on her. "All I can say now is that I've found love in a rather unusual place."

"Yeah, it might hurt at first back there, but you get used to it," Tony responds.

"What is he?" Anya asks. "Age appropriate? Employed?"

"A legal citizen?" Sven adds.

"Sven!" Anya cries out.

"That was one time," Heather mutters, defending herself. "Why does everyone keep throwing Diego in my face?"

Sven leans over to Nathan and whispers. "I don't think he needed to be thrown there, if you know what I'm saying."

That causes Nathan to look over at Tony, who smiles mischievously at him. And of course, Gunn notices Nathan noticing Tony, and he reaches for his recently filled wineglass.

Tony mimics the move, raising his wineglass in the air. "I'd like to propose a toast."

Everyone raises their glasses and awaits the toast.

Tony stands. "To the poster boys for gay marriage."

Nathan clears his throat. "Marriage equality."

"I stand corrected," Tony says with a slight bow in Nathan's direction. "Marriage equality. And may your marriage be equal in happiness to those of your parents."

Martha smirks and downs her glass of wine.

Anya stares across the table at Sven and puts her wineglass down, untasted.

Still standing, Tony holds out his glass. "To the happy couple." He drinks and sits.

Gunn and Nathan sip unenthusiastically from their wineglasses, as Heather looks around the table, confused.

Anya leans toward her son. "Who exactly is that?"

Gunn stares daggers at Tony. "He's trouble, which starts with T, which rhymes with P, which stands for Pri..."

"Olaf!" Anya interrupts him before he can finish the word.

Nathan throws his napkin on the table. "Mother, can I talk to you for a second?" He walks through the restaurant and out the front door.

"Excuse me." Martha stands and follows her son.

Another awkward silence consumes the table.

"I'm going to visit the little girls' room," Heather announces politely. "Anya, dear, why don't you join me?"

"I'm good," Anya says, crunching on a breadstick and staring at Sven.

"Come with me anyway," Heather suggests, a little more forcefully.

"Why?" Anya asks, clueless.

Heather stands and walks around to pull out Anya's chair. "Oh, for goodness sake. Just come with me." She drags Anya in the direction of the restrooms.

Gunn pulls his cell phone out of his pocket. "I need to make a call." He walks towards the restaurant's side patio.

That leaves just Tony and Sven at the table. In silence.

Finally, Sven asks, "So, Tony, do you have a girlfriend?"

* * *

In the ladies' restroom, Anya splashes water on her face and dries it off with a paper towel, as Heather steps out of a stall and washes her hands.

"Enough is enough, Anya," Heather declares. "You have to tell me what's wrong with you. Or what's wrong with Sven."

That causes Anya's lower lip to start trembling as her eyes start watering. "I don't know what to do," Anya cries.

"About what?" Heather puts a comforting hand on Anya's shoulder. "Did Sven do something?"

Anya sniffles. "Like what?"

"I don't know," Heather says, grasping at straws. "Did he… did he cheat on you?"

Anya gasps then slaps Heather's hand away from her. "How dare you! Ah, jeez, Sven would never do that! Why would you say something like that?"

"With the way you've been acting, I…" Heather steps back. "I've never seen you this angry with Sven. You're not yourself. Why, I walked in on Sven totally naked the other night, and you didn't even say a word."

Heather crosses her arms. "I miss our little back-and-forth Krystal-and-Alexis jabs. Even if we didn't really mean them."

Anya wipes her eyes. "Who said I didn't mean them, you… you… you trollop?"

"Trollop?" Heather laughs.

"I'm out of practice," Anya concedes. "Unlike your bed."

That makes Heather smile. "That's better. Unlike that hideous sweater you're wearing. Did you lose a contest or something?"

Anya finally smiles through her tears. "Good times."

"Now, will you tell me what's wrong?"

Anya checks her makeup in the bathroom mirror. "Soon. You'll know soon."

* * *

On the restaurant's patio, Gunn dials Abby's number, but no one answers. He gets her outgoing message.

"This is Abby. If you're hearing this, why aren't you sending me a text? Who leaves voice mails anymore? I guess if you do, wait for the beep."

The beep sounds, and Gunn speaks.

"Why aren't you here, Abby? I need to talk to you. I need to talk to someone. Nathan's first boyfriend showed up, long story, and I can tell there's still something between them. I saw them kissing, and then..." He hesitates. "Well, I'll can't tell you what happened next on the phone."

He scratches his head with his free hand.

"And my mom's acting weird, and Nathan's mom's acting weird, and his dad isn't even here."

He looks over and sees Nathan and Martha talking outside the restaurant's front door.

"Am I doing the right thing? I mean, is marriage the right thing? I know we deserve it, like everyone does, but just because we can get married, should we? It's so heteronormative. And if one more person asks which one of us is the bride, I'm gonna scream!

"And what are my parents going to think about that other thing? We haven't told them, and I don't want to tell them unless it's definitely going to happen, and I don't know how they're going to react."

Gunn sighs. "Get here soon, Abby."

* * *

In front of the restaurant, Nathan argues with his mother. "You have to tell me where Dad is."

"I told you," Martha replies, but her tone seems evasive.

"Why does your tone sound evasive?" Nathan asks.

"Just know that he wanted to be here. He really did."

"Then why isn't he?" Nathan demands.

"Because," Martha stammers, "because…"

She sits on one of the benches near the restaurant's valet stand.

"Because he's in custody. Police custody," Martha confesses with a sigh. "He was arrested last week. He's in jail."

"What?" Nathan cries in surprise as he sits next to his mother.

"His business partners weren't entirely..." Martha hesitates. "Their dealings weren't entirely legal. Not always. And it looks like your father is taking the fall."

"I don't believe it," Nathan says, and he doesn't. Maybe in the back of his mind, he had suspected that some of his father's colleagues, primarily the ones from Italy, might not be exactly who they claimed to be, but then he reprimanded himself for buying into the Italian mafia stereotype. He never really believed his father was part of that business.

"I don't believe it, either, sweetheart," Martha reassures him, "but there wasn't anything I could do there."

She takes one of Nathan's hands in hers. "Your father insisted that I come to the wedding. And he did want to be here. He really did. I feel terrible not being there with him, but I couldn't forgive myself if I wasn't here with you."

"Can I talk to him?" Nathan asks.

Martha shakes her head. "Not right now. Trust me, darling, I didn't want to tell you, not before the wedding."

"I can't even think about the wedding right now," Nathan states. "And why did you bring <u>him</u>?"

"Anthony?" Martha inquires. "I told you. He's my assistant at the gallery."

"Mom! We didn't just know each other in high school. We <u>knew</u> each other in high school, and now he's trying to break me and Gunn up." Nathan looks at her to see if she understood.

Martha narrows her eyes in confusion, then opens them wide in realization. "Oh! He's that Tony. I had no idea!"

Nathan shakes his head. "Well, you didn't pay much attention to me back then."

Martha puts an arm around her son. "I'm sorry for that. And I'm sorry for this, but you have to believe me, I didn't know he was going to try anything like that."

Nathan stands, pacing. "What can I do? For Dad. For you."

"Just get married and be happy."

Nathan sighs. "I wonder if that's even possible now."

Chapter 15

The ride home from the restaurant was silent, with Gunn being upset with Nathan, and with Nathan being upset with Tony and with his dad's situation. Tony, meanwhile, relished every moment of the ride.

When the trio arrives at the rental house, Nathan pulls Gunn into the first-floor home office, closes the door, and proceeds to tell him everything he knew about his father's arrest, which isn't much.

Gunn fires up his laptop and does several searches for any news about Peter Stanford, but comes up empty handed.

"That's good, right?" Gunn asks, sitting behind his desk, peering at the computer screen. "I mean, if it was something major, it certainly would have made the news."

Nathan shrugs as he sits down in one of the room's small armchairs. "You know, I didn't like the man for most of my youth, but I really can't picture him breaking the law or being part of the mafia."

"Of course not," Gunn agrees.

"I mean, he owns his own construction company. In New Jersey. And he has investors in Italy." Nathan pauses and thinks about what he just said. "Oh, for crying in the sink! My dad's in the mob!"

Normally, Gunn would compliment Nathan on his proper use of "for crying in the sink," but this really isn't the time for that.

"Does your mom know what the charges are?"

Nathan shakes his head. "She didn't say. Only that he was arrested at his office early last week."

"Why didn't she tell you?"

"She says that she was hoping that it was a mistake, that he would be released in time for the wedding, blah blah blah," Nathan says, rubbing his eyes in frustration. "She probably thinks I can't handle it."

"But you can," Gunn tries to reassure him, but Nathan looks at him like he's crazy.

"Are you kidding? I can't handle this! Not days before our wedding! I'm stressed out enough as it is!"

"You didn't seem stressed out before Tony got here," Gunn quips.

Nathan tilts his head and stares at Gunn. "A, that's not fair. And B, of course I was stressed out. Getting married is one of the most stressful things you can do in life."

"Yeah," Gunn responds, "if you want to get married, that is." He pauses. "Do you? Do you still want to get married? To me?"

"How can you even ask that?" Nathan exclaims.

"Well, you were kissing Tony in the steam room," Gunn says pointedly.

"It was a <u>sauna</u>!" Nathan yells. "And he kissed me, not the other way around."

"You looked like you were enjoying it."

"It lasted a second. I was waiting for you, and he came in and surprised me."

"What if I hadn't walked in?"

"But you did, Blanche. You did." Nathan tries a different tactic. "What if the attendant hadn't walked in? Huh?"

"Huh?" Gunn seems confused by the question.

"What would you have done? Did you want to take Tony up on his offer?"

"No!"

"It's okay if you did. I mean, it wouldn't be the first time."

Gunn opens his mouth to respond, to deny it, but he knows it wouldn't be true. Sophomore year. Spring Break. Fort Lauderdale. They had been in their second year of dating, and Gunn had realized how much more experience Nathan had with, as he put it at the time, "the gay stuff." And so, when the opportunity had presented itself in the form of Chuck, a junior from UT-Austin, he and Nathan had talked about it, and talked about it, and talked about it some more, before they spent two interesting nights with Chuck. Gunn remembers now that

Nathan had talked about being tri-curious in high school, and now he realizes that Tony had been part of that curious equation.

"Is that what you want?" Gunn asks. "Is monogamy just another straight concept that our community has co-opted because we feel like it's what we're supposed to do?"

"Why are you talking about 'our community' right now?" Nathan screams back at him. "We're talking about us. You and me."

"Because I'm not crazy. I've seen the way you look at Tony. And I can't blame you. I mean, he's super tall and I'm, come on, look at me," Gunn gestures to his short frame. "He has, like, no body fat, and I'm worried every day that I'm gonna turn into my mother. And he used to be a freakin' model! I can't compete with that," Gunn says, defeated.

"I never asked you to compete with that," Nathan replies. "But obviously you've been checking him out. Should I be worried?"

"No!" Gunn yells. "I don't want a tall, handsome model with a full head of hair. I want you."

"You never mentioned his hair before," Nathan gasps.

"I know, and I realized that mistake as soon as I said it," Gunn yells.

They fall silent, their anger running out of steam. They stare at each other, breathing hard.

"So you didn't kiss him?" Gunn asks.

"No. He kissed me," Nathan answers.

"And you don't want to..." Gunn leaves the question open.

Nathan shakes his head. "Only with you."

"Are you sure?"

Nathan stares at Gunn, love in his eyes, but his response is pure sarcasm. "Unless John Barrowman shows up, and then you're on your own."

Gunn chuckles at that. "Count me in on that."

Suddenly, Tony's voice booms through the office door. "I've been told I look like John Barrowman where it counts."

Nathan and Gunn look at the door, then Nathan walks over and opens it. Tony stands there, a huge grin on his face – and nothing else on his body.

Nathan gestures at Tony's naked body with exasperation, then looks over at Gunn. "It's like living with your father."

"Yeah, Gunn, your dad is hot!"

Gunn rolls his eyes. If he had a dollar for every time he heard that...

"And I actually have four percent body fat, but who's counting."

Gunn stands and pushes his way past Tony, and Nathan immediately follows.

Tony calls after them, "So when should I expect you guys?"

Chapter 16

The doorbell never stops ringing at the Gunnunderson houses the next day.

A rush of last-minute gifts are delivered by FedEx, UPS, and the regular mailman at Gunn and Nathan's house. Gunn leaves early in the morning to visit his parents and their various family members coming in that day, leaving Nathan to hold down the fort, accept and track the wedding presents, and go over a few last-minute details with Heather.

For better or worse, Martha decided to join them, as well. Nathan had hoped to send Tony over to his mother's hotel suite under the pretense of helping her with work for her art gallery, but that hope was dashed when she arrived unexpectedly and proceeded to second guess many of Nathan's decisions.

"Wouldn't a bright red boutonnière look more festival than a white one?" she asks as she sips on her second bloody Mary of the morning. "Something with green leaves. Red and green, for your Christmas theme!"

"It's not a completely Christmas-themed wedding, Mother," Nathan explains for the hundredth time. "It's a wedding at Christmas."

"What about the reception?"

Nathan sighs. "Okay, yes. That is Christmas themed."

"But it's more on the silver-and-blue end of the Christmas color scheme instead of traditional red-and-green," Heather reminds them.

"So it's more of a Hanukkah-themed Christmas-themed reception?" Martha asks pointedly at Heather.

Heather takes a beat, staring at Martha, before gesturing at her drink. "Are there any more of those?"

"In the kitchen, dear," Martha nods in that direction. "A whole pitcher in the refrigerator."

Heather leaves them and goes into the kitchen.

"Be nice, Mother," Nathan begs.

"I am being nice, darling," Martha feigns innocently. "But a Christmas-themed reception? It's not going to look like ... their house, is it?"

"Whose house?"

"You know very well whose house I'm talking about. Anya. Sven. The Gunnundersons. That Christmas explosion she calls decorations."

Nathan thinks about their house for a moment. "Maybe it's a little over the top."

Martha chortles as she takes another drink of her bloody Mary.

"Not everyone can be content with a simple wire sculpture in the shape of Christmas tree," he adds, thinking of his parents' traditional holiday decorations.

"Simple?" Martha gasps. "That sculpture was one of the first pieces I acquired when I opened the Martha Stanford Gallery. The artist has gone on to create large-form sculptures for some of the biggest buildings in New York. She's been shown at the finest museums, including the National Museum of Women in the Arts in Washington, D.C."

Nathan rolls his eyes.

"That tree that you apparently despise is now worth $75,000," Martha adds.

Nathan drops the pen he's holding. "Are you serious?"

Martha nods.

Nathan blinks, then points to his dining table.

"It would look amazing over there," Nathan suggests all too casually. "You know, if you wanted to give us a last-minute present."

Mother and son stare at each other, then burst into laughter.

After the laughter subsides, Martha says, "Sometimes, Nathan, I feel like I hardly know you, and then sometimes, you sound just like that little boy who liked to put on shows in the media room."

"Oh, please do not tell Gunn about those shows."

"I remember one. You were dancing to that obscene singer's video, and you would put your hands up on the side of your head, like this."

Martha places her hands in L-shapes on either side of her beautiful red hair.

Nathan laughs again. "Vogue. Oh, yes. My Madonna period." He sighs and then frowns. "Father hated that."

"He didn't know what to do with you, Nathan. Neither did I, to be honest," Martha confesses.

"I know."

"We were raised differently, Nathan. We didn't expect to have a son who was ... like you."

"Yeah, I'm a little too fabulous for most people," Nathan retorts. He starts to say something else, but then stops. It's not that he doesn't want to talk to his mother about his childhood, about his sexuality, about all the things in his life that shaped the man he had become. But with his dad being arrested, his ex-boyfriend showing up, and the general craziness of the past week, he didn't feel like going down that road. Not today.

"Whatever happened to that singer?"

"Who? Madonna?" Nathan asks.

"Yes. Is she anybody now? Maybe we could get her to perform at your wedding," Martha suggests.

"You do that, Mother. You do that."

* * *

In the kitchen, Heather puts the final touches on her bloody Mary – a splash of Tabasco stirred in with a celery stalk – when Tony comes in the back door, obviously back from a run.

Tony wears just a pair of running shorts apart from his shoes and socks. Sweat pours down his face and his smooth chest.

"Hey there, Mrs. Mancuso," he says, out of breath.

Heather sips her drink as she checks out Tony, head to toe. "I told you, Tony, call me…" She thinks about it for a second. "Actually, Mrs. Mancuso is fine."

Tony grabs a cup towel off the kitchen country and dabs his face with it. "Where's Nathan?"

"In the living room with his mother."

"Isn't that sweet," Tony replies as he uses the towel to wipe the sweat from his chest.

"Actually, Tony, it is sweet," Heather states emphatically as she takes a step toward Tony. "Nathan is a good kid, and it's lovely to see him spending time with his mother, and seeing her get to know him better. Not that you would know anything about that. You're here instead of spending Christmas with your own parents. Why is that?"

"Actually, Mrs. Mancuso, my parents were killed in a car wreck a few years ago."

"Oh!" That silences Heather.

"I did visit their graves before we left to come here, if that makes you feel any better."

Heather shakes her head. "No, it doesn't. It makes me feel horrible for acting that way. I'm sorry."

"That's okay. I'm used to people underestimating me."

"People like Nathan?"

"People like Gunn. He shouldn't underestimate me when it comes to knowing what Nathan needs."

"Don't you dare ..." Heather starts to say something before Tony interrupts her.

"Speaking of children and parents, where is your daughter these days? Gabby, isn't it?"

That really puts Heather on the defensive. "Abby. She's on her way home. She's going to be here for the wedding."

"And if there wasn't a wedding? Would she be here for Christmas?"

Heather takes a step back. "She lives in North Carolina. It's a long way to travel, and it's so hard during the holidays, especially with her family and everything."

"I guess she could always make the effort. If she wanted to."

Heather narrows her eyes and steps close to Tony, grabbing the cup towel out of his hand.

"I think you'd better go clean up, young man."

"Are you sure?" Tony asks. "I heard you like young men."

"Not anymore, and certainly not you."

Tony blows a kiss in Heather's direction before leaving the kitchen.

When he's gone, Heather clears her throat and takes another sip of her drink. "Ten years ago, I would have eaten you for lunch, little boy."

* * *

"For the rehearsal dinner, I found the loveliest Alexander McQueen jumpsuit in a deep green that looks simply stunning with my hair, if I do say so myself. You remember that emerald necklace your father gave me for our 25th anniversary?" Martha stops her glowing description of her outfits to wait for Nathan's response.

Nathan nods. "I do. It's beautiful."

"Yes, it is. So that's for the rehearsal dinner."

"Shoes?" Nathan asks.

"Jimmy Choo, the ones I bought on your last visit to Manhattan."

"Nice." Nathan nods his approval.

"And for the wedding itself..." Martha clutches a hand to her chest and gasps. "Honey, I think I've outdone myself."

"Oh, please tell me you have a homemade pink prom dress made out of your mother's homemade pink prom dress and you're going to wear it even though you've always been told than redheads shouldn't wear pink."

Martha pauses and stares at Nathan. "Have you hit your head, darling?"

Nathan shakes his head and smiles. "Sorry. *Pretty In Pink*. It's a movie."

Martha rolls her eyes, but in a kind way. "Anyway, it's not pink. It's red. Stunning. Floor length. Michael Costello."

"Ooh, I love him!"

"I know, darling. I searched him out based on your recommendation."

"And Anya's wearing green, so there's your traditional Christmas red and green."

"Perfect!" Martha finishes off her bloody Mary. "It looks so good with your father's family tartan kilt." She sighs, and the joy leaves her face. "I'm so worried about him, sweetheart."

Nathan reaches out and takes his mother's hand. "Me, too, Mom. Is there anything I can do?"

She shakes her head. "I talked to our attorney this morning, but he can't learn anything. I don't know. Maybe your father instructed him not to tell me anything."

Nathan hesitates before asking his next question, the one that's been on his mind ever since he heard the news about his father. "Do you think he did it? Do you think he's guilty of whatever they're charging him with?"

Martha tries to delay answering him by reaching for her drink, but finding it empty, she takes a deep breath and answers. "I know your father, and I don't believe he would knowingly do anything illegal. But ..."

"But what?" Nathan inquires.

"But I've never trusted some of his business associates," Martha confesses. "Some of them just give me a bad feeling when I'm around them. It's hard to explain."

"I remember a group of men coming to the house when I was maybe sixteen or seventeen. They shut themselves away in Father's study for two days, and you made me stay at a friend's house while they were there. Something about that always bothered me."

"I remember that!" Martha's face wrinkles in remembrance. "Those are exactly the people I didn't like. I never trusted them. Maybe your father trusted them too much." She looks at Nathan. "I'm surprised you remembered that."

Nathan smiles in response. "Of course, I remember it. It was the first time I stayed over at ..." He pauses.

"Stayed over where, dear?"

Suddenly, Tony's voice booms out from the dining room. "My house. It was the first time he stayed over at my house."

Nathan and Martha look over at Tony, still shirtless from his run and still brazen from his encounter with Heather in the kitchen.

"I remember that weekend very well, Nathan," Tony adds.

Martha looks back and forth from Tony to Nathan. "Oh!" she exclaims. "I see."

"Did you have a nice run?" Nathan asks, trying to change the subject.

"Very. I'm loving the warm weather here. It was freezing back home."

"Yeah, you probably had to wear clothes and everything," Nathan comments.

"Not if I can help it," Tony responds with a wink.

Martha clears her throat in obvious embarrassment, but before she can say anything, the doorbell rings.

Nathan groans. "Not another delivery."

"I'll get it," Tony offers as he walks to the front door and opens it.

But it's not a delivery person at the door.

It's Thomas.

Thomas whistles as he checks out Tony's chest, abs, and everything else.

Tony smiles seductively as he returns the once-over. "Can I help you?" He spies the suitcase at Thomas's feet. "Lend you a hand?"

"If there's any justice in this world," Thomas replies, licking his lips.

"Thomas? Is that you?" Nathan calls out upon hearing his best friend's voice. He bounds to the front door and gives Thomas a big hug.

"You made it!" Nathan cries.

"I made it!" Thomas responds, as the two of them continue the warm hug.

"I made it, too," Tony adds. "Can I join in?"

Nathan shoots daggers at Tony with his eyes, but Thomas thinks about the offer, raising his eyebrows.

"That must be Tony," Thomas states, clearly having been informed about the surprise visitor.

"That must be Tony," Nathan agrees.

"And you are…?" Tony asks.

"Thomas. Thomas Krickstein."

Suddenly, a look of realization and disappointment crosses Nathan's face.

"And Tony is staying in our guest room, where you're supposed to be staying. God, I'm sorry. I didn't even think this through."

"Bitch! That's it. I'm going home," Thomas replies playfully.

"I'm happy to share," Tony offers, even more playfully. He and Thomas share a look and a mischievous smile that Nathan totally misses.

"Down, girl," Nathan says to Tony.

"I can sleep on the couch," Thomas offers to Nathan, then turns to Tony. "I've slept in worse places."

"Speaking of, where's Daniel?" He turns to Tony. "Daniel is his boyfriend."

"Daniel's not my boyfriend," Thomas corrects him.

"What?" Nathan exclaims in surprise.

"We broke up."

"Again?"

"Again." Thomas pouts, but he doesn't seem too surprised or upset. "Long story."

"I'm sorry, Thomas."

"I expect him to call any minute now and apologize."

"As usual."

"As usual," Thomas responds with resignation. They've clearly been down this road before. "Maybe he'll even show up for the wedding."

"I hope so, man." Nathan puts a comforting hand on Thomas's shoulder. "In the meantime…"

"I can sleep on the couch. There's no need to change anyone else's plans."

"If you're sure…" Nathan says, looking for any chance to change Tony's plans.

"I'll be fine."

"Do you need to freshen up?" Tony asks of Thomas. "I was about to take a shower if you want to…"

"If you want to come say hello to my mother," Nathan interrupts.

"Love to," Thomas responds.

Nathan takes him inside and calls back to Tony, "Bring his bag inside, won't you?"

Chapter 17

Meanwhile, at Sven and Anya's house, the party is just getting started with the arrival of Anya's family from Wisconsin, the Gundersons. Yes, Anya's maiden name was Gunderson, which led to all kinds of confusion and jokes when she married a Gunnunderson.

Anya's identical twin sister, Tanya, had finally made it to town early that morning with their mother, Olivia.

"Good golly, we would have picked you up at the airport, dontcha know!" Anya screams as she embraces Tanya.

"And miss the chance to drive where there's no snow in the winter?" Tanya screams in response. "Not on your ever-loving life!"

And with that, the giggling starts. In stereo.

"You gonna ignore your old mom here?" Olivia cries out.

"Mama!" Anya cries out as she wraps her arms around her mother. Well, as far as they will go.

"There's my baby girl!" Olivia says as she kisses Anya on the cheek.

"Oh, now, Mom!"

"Don't you 'Oh, now, Mom' me! You'll always be my baby girl, and don't you forget it!"

"What am I?" Tanya asks playfully. "Pickled herring?"

"You're the older sister," Anya says, poking her twin in the shoulder, "and don't you ever forget it."

"Older, for crying in the sink! I'm four frickin' minutes older!" Tanya defends herself.

"Ah, jeez. I can see those older sister laugh lines around your eyes," Anya jokes.

"Guilty as charged!" Tanya responds. And if the giggling could get any louder, it does.

Together, the three Gunderson women look more like triplets than a mother and two daughters. The same round figure. The same beautiful face. The same kind eyes. And definitely the same voice.

"Come on into the kitchen, why dontcha?" Anya demands. "Leave your bags at the door. Sven can get them later."

"Where is that tall Minnesotan drink of water?" Tanya asks.

"Don't know. Don't care," Anya states as she leads them into the kitchen and pours coffee for all three of them.

Tanya and Olivia share a look.

"What's wrong, baby girl?" Olivia asks, maternal concern on her face.

"Nothing," Anya responds unconvincingly. "It's just..."

Her lower lip starts to quiver. Tanya recognizes that sign.

"Oh, no, Mama! Here come the gosh darn waterworks!"

And she's right. Anya starts to cry while trying to explain herself.

"It's just that… I tried to… And he…" Nothing she says is remotely understandable, but her sister and mother surround her and hug her anyway.

"It's okay, baby girl," Olivia comforts her.

"No, it's not!" Anya blubbers. "I'm…"

Before she can finish, Sven comes out of the basement.

"Hey, hey, it's the Gundersons!" he starts to sing, but he quickly stops when Olivia and Tanya form a barrier between him and Anya. "What's going on here?"

"As if you didn't know," Olivia says, accusation in her voice.

"I don't know!" Sven counters. "She's been like this for days, dontcha know. Crying for no reason. Treating me like I took the last bratwurst at the family barbecue without asking first."

Olivia and Tanya gasp in unison. "You didn't!" Tanya asks.

"No, I didn't!" Sven states before stopping, looking back and forth at nothing in particular, then staring into space. "Or did I?"

"It's not about your darn bratwurst!" Anya cries out. "You know what it's about."

"On the grave of Brett Favre, I don't, Mama!"

Anya squints her eyes. "Brett Favre isn't dead, Papa!"

Sven has to think about that for a few seconds. "Then why did I send that edible basket to his family?"

Anya sighs. "I don't know, but I'm sure they enjoyed receiving a nice fruit basket out of the blue like that."

"Oh, it wasn't that kind of edible basket," Sven confesses.

Just then, Gunn steps out of the basement. He stops and quickly closes his mouth when he sees his grandmother and aunt.

Olivia and Tanya squeal in unison. "Olaf!"

Gunn holds his breath as long as he can, then coughs, a large cloud of smoke expelling from his lungs. "Grandma! Aunt Tanya! Merry Christmas!"

The two women rush over to hug him, pushing Sven out of the way in the process. They muss Gunn's hair, pinch his cheeks, and generally act the way older relatives do at Christmas.

"I can't believe you're getting married!" Olivia exclaims.

"I can't believe you're old enough to get married!" Tanya counters.

"I can't believe you're getting married to another man!" Olivia adds.

"I can't believe it's legal for you to get married to another man!" Tanya states.

"It is, and I am," Gunn responds. "And I'm glad you could make it."

"Like we'd miss it!" Olivia sounds insulted.

"Just try to stop us!" Tanya screams out.

Olivia and Tanya look at each other and giggle. Loudly.

Gunn's eyes bug out at the sound. "Wow! That is…" He can't even describe it. "Wow!"

Olivia stares at Gunn, her expression turning serious. "You look more and more like your Grandpa Dick every time I see you." She turns to Anya. "Doesn't he look like a little Dick to you?"

Anya surveys her son. "Now that you mention it…"

Olivia interrupts her. "If you came to visit us up in Wisconsin more often, young man, oh, all the relatives up there would say you're the spitting image of Dick."

"I have a great idea!" Tanya cries out. "Come up to Wisconsin on your honeymoon, why dontcha! You might even be able to see the Packers in the playoffs."

Gunn doesn't now how to respond. "As much as I enjoy seeing a good group of Packers, we're going to Hawaii for the honeymoon and New Year's Eve."

"Christ on a cookie, that sounds like fun!" Tanya turns to Anya. "You guys should go with them!"

Anya looks away from Sven's general direction. "I don't think so."

Suddenly, Tanya remembers the fight between Anya and Sven. "Well, you don't have to take Sven if you don't want to."

"Um, I'm right here," Sven interjects.

"Then don't be," Tanya responds.

Sven shakes his head in confusion and heads into the living room.

"Mom, you have to make up with Dad," Gunn says with frustration. "At least tell me what's going on."

"Pish posh! You have your wedding to deal with. I can deal with your father," Anya says, waving her hands in the air as if to change the subject.

"Are you staying in my old room?" Gunn asks of his relatives. "With the bunk beds?"

"We are," Olivia replies. "We flipped a coin, and I won, so I get to be on top." She pauses, looks into space, deep in thought, and sighs. "I do miss my Dick."

* * *

By lunchtime, the small family contingent from St. Paul had arrived – Sven's parents, Gustav and Elsa Gunnunderson, along with Elsa's nephew, Jasper Jorgenson. After an enormous meal prepared by Tanya and Olivia, the two families relax in the living room, which barely has room for all of them between the numerous Christmas trees, presents and decorations. In fact, some people have to sit at the dining table or pull chairs from the table into the living room to sit.

As the two families reacquaint themselves, Gunn sits quietly, looking at the people who were literally responsible for his existence.

Unlike so many of his friends, Gunn doesn't have a large extended family – no siblings, no cousins his age to play with at family gatherings, no distant relation to inherit an unknown fortune from in the future. His father's only sibling, his identical twin Olaf, had passed away when they were boys, leaving a giant hole in Sven's life and, as Gunn learned later, discouraging Sven's parents from having any more children. His paternal grandfather, Gustav, has no siblings, and his paternal grandmother, Elsa, had had one brother, Jasper, whose single son is with them now. Gunn had often wondered how someone could go through life with the name of Jasper Jorgenson, Jr., but then he remembers his own moniker, Olaf Erick Gunnunderson, and considers Jasper to be the fortunate one.

His mother has just the only sister, Tanya, also an identical twin. While Anya married Sven just after high school, Tanya had remained single. She repeatedly says that she didn't need a man in her life to make her happy (or a woman, when Gunn asked her that question the year after he had come out to his parents). She seems perfectly content with her life, which makes Gunn happy to hear.

He had never known Richard Gunderson (better known as Dick), his grandfather on his mother's side, who had passed away when Gunn was less than a year old. Even though Olivia had been young when her husband died, she never looked at another man her entire life. She says that true love lasts a lifetime, even if her lifetime lasted longer than his.

With three living grandparents, Gunn considers himself lucky, especially since all of Nathan's grandparents were deceased. Nathan's parents also had been only children, which perhaps explains their rationale for only having one child. Gunn's courses in psychology also taught him that this might also explain their coldness to Nathan when he was growing up, their inability to share and be warm with their only son. Or maybe there were other reasons.

Gunn doesn't know if his parents and Nathan's parents would ever be close. They had certainly come a long way from their first meeting, when Sven and Anya had come to Manhattan to visit Gunn and Nathan. The Stanfords had come in from New Jersey to meet the Gunnundersons, and while it wasn't the train wreck that Gunn and Nathan expected, they hadn't exactly turned out to be best friends, either.

In other words, they had a fairly typical in-law relationship. Watching his own grandparents interact today,

Gunn realizes that the Gunnundersons and the Gundersons probably had the same relationship – cordial but not a "let's all go on vacation together!" friendship. Still, Gunn likes seeing what Gustav Gunnunderson referred to as the "younger generation" (which consisted solely of Tanya and Jasper) getting along.

Gunn is startled out of his reverie by a question from Granddad Gunnunderson.

"Olaf, did you get our wedding present?"

Gunn nods. "I did, but we aren't opening anything until after we get back from Hawaii, so don't tell me what it is."

"Well, we found it on your registry. What's the name of that website? The Danube? The Sahara? Something like that."

"I think you mean Amazon," Gunn suggests.

Gustav snaps his fingers. "That's it!"

"Oh, ignore him," Elsa chimes in. "He knows exactly what it is. He loves his Kindle, dontcha know. Uses it all the gall-darn time!"

"And it's a little different than when I caught our Sven playing with his Kindle when he was a teenager, if you know what I'm saying."

That gets a rousing laugh from everyone except for Anya, who silently sips at her tea.

"That's something that runs in the family," Sven adds, pointing at Gunn. "If those bunk beds could talk, oh boy!"

That even gets a smile from Anya, while Gunn shakes his head, embarrassed. "Can we change the subject, please?"

"Oh, we're just playing around," Gustav replies.

"So was he," Sven adds with a chuckle.

"I guess that's something you'll miss out on," Gustav adds offhandedly.

Gunn looks at him, confused. "What do you mean?"

"Well, it's just something that's shared between fathers and sons, and you..." He lets the sentence go unfinished.

"We can have kids, Granddad," Gunn replies.

"Now, I know things have changed these days, but they haven't changed that much, that's for sure."

"We can adopt," Gunn says with a little too much determination. "We can foster kids. We could even have our own kids through in vitro fertilization."

That gets Anya's attention. "Wait a minute, young man. Have you and Nathan talked about having kids?"

Gunn hesitates, feeling everyone's eyes on him. "We've talked about it. We both want kids. I think. Someday."

"When?" Anya asks. "Soon?"

"Let's get through the wedding first, okay?" Gunn tries to defuse the situation.

"Oh, my goodness gracious," Anya cries out. "I'm going to be a grandmother!" She stops and thinks about that realization for a second, then she starts to really cry. Again.

"I'm going to be a grandmother?" And soon she's gasping for air between words. "I'm! Not! Old! Enough! To! Be! A! Grandmother!"

Olivia wraps her arm around her daughter's shoulder. "It's okay, dear. I was younger than you are now when I became a grandmother."

Anya looks at her mother's face, and then lets out a ridiculously loud cry.

"Well!" Olivia declares. "I'll try not to take that personally!"

* * *

Later that night, after Sven got his parents and cousin checked in at their hotel, and everyone from all the families had enjoyed a long and very loud dinner at Gunn and Nathan's house, the couple lay in bed next to each other, recapping their day.

"Thomas looks good," Gunn comments. "It's a shame about him and Daniel, though."

"Oh, please," Nathan responds. "They'll be back together before New Year's Eve."

Gunn chuckles. "Probably. Any word on the soloist?"

"Just that she's battling a sore throat. Heather's already working on finding a replacement."

"That sucks. She is so good."

"What do we do if we can't find a replacement?" Nathan asks.

"We'll find a replacement," Gunn insists.

"But if we don't?"

Gunn shrugs. "Then we drop it from the service."

Nathan looks surprised. "Just like that?"

"Just like that." Gunn notices Nathan's look. "What?"

"You fought tooth and nail to have that in our wedding. And you're not even religious."

"Hey, I like *Ave Maria*. It's pretty."

Nathan thinks about it. "I think those are the words when they're translated. 'That Maria, she so pretty.' I think it was the basis for *West Side Story*."

"I like the idea of having a super religious hymn at a gay wedding. I really like the idea of religious nutjobs going insane over having a super religious hymn at a gay wedding."

"I thought our position is that this isn't a gay wedding, it's just a wedding. With two men. Who happen to be gay."

"That's our official position," Gunn responds. "Our realistic position is that it's a bloody gay wedding."

"The rainbow and unicorn centerpieces certainly make that case."

They sit in silence for a few minutes before Gunn brings up a new topic.

"So… Long story, but my mother kind of asked if we're planning on having kids.

"Why? When?" Nathan asks, shocked.

"This afternoon when my parents' families came in."

"How did it come up?"

"We were talking about teenage masturbation," Gunn replies.

"As you do…" Nathan closes one eye as he tries to imagine that conversation. "What did you tell her?"

"Just that we've talked about it and that we want kids."

"Is it cliché?"

"To want kids?"

"For a gay couple to want kids. Part of me feels like every gay couple these days has a kid. Like the baby comes free with purchase at Restoration Hardware," says Nathan. "And frankly, for what they charge for an L-shaped leather sofa, they should throw in a baby for fee. Or at least a set of floor lamps."

"We've talked about this, Nathan. Are you changing your mind?"

"No. Not really. It's just…" He looks over at Gunn. "You know my parents. That's the example I was raised with. Is that the kind of father I'm going to be?"

"Do you think I'm going to be a stoner dad like my dad?"

"I wish," Nathan jokes.

"I'm serious."

Nathan rolls over onto his side to face his fiancé.

"I don't think we're destined to be like our parents any more than we're destined to be like every other gay couple, or like you're destined to be like every other philosophy professor, or like I'm destined to be like every other devastatingly handsome yet unusually short Italian-Scottish-English-Canadian hybrid."

"I think you might be the only one of those. And I'm glad you're short."

"I know. You've said. It makes our naughty parts fit together better."

"I don't think those were my exact words."

Nathan nods. "Picture it. Sophomore year. Fall semester. The bathroom on the fourth floor of the main library after the homecoming football game."

Gunn smiles as he remembers. "Oh, yeah. Naughty parts. I did say that."

"And we're a little off the subject."

"Kids."

"Kids."

"You'll make a great dad, Nathan."

"And you'll make a great mom, Gunn."

Gunn sighs. "You know how I hate using gender-specific nomenclature for roles in same-sex relationships. It's demeaning and perpetuates negative stereotypes of gay men as weak and effeminate, and it discourages people from viewing gay men in relationships as being equals."

Nathan stares at Gunn. "Is it your time of the month?"

Before Gunn can respond, there's a knock on the door.

Gunn and Nathan look at each other and then shout in unison, "Go away!"

But it's not Tony's voice that answers. It's a quiet voice with an English accent. "But Papa, I cannot sleep, and I fear the wolves will spirit me away in the night."

Nathan rolls his eyes. "Come in, Thomas."

The door opens and Thomas steps in sheepishly, wearing boxer briefs and a tank top. He smiles at the couple in bed. "Whatcha doing?"

"Washing an elephant," Gunn replies.

"Well, that's a new name for it," Thomas says as he closes the door behind him. "Make room." He gets under the covers next to Nathan, who moves to the center of the bed, closer to Gunn.

Thomas looks under the covers with a gasp. "You boys are naked!"

Nathan pushes the covers down. "Is the couch that bad?"

Thomas shrugs. "No, I just didn't get to visit with you guys enough today. And soon you'll be married and you won't have any time for your single friends like me. Those of us without a boyfriend to come with them to a friend's wedding."

"So, what happened with Daniel?" Gunn asks with a sigh.

Thomas rolls his eyes with a huff. "He started to feel guilty that he wasn't going to spend Christmas with his mother. Who, incidentally, doesn't know he's gay."

"How is that even possible?" Nathan asks.

"I know, right?" Thomas replies. "But I don't want to talk about him. I want to talk about you. Do you think Daniel is right for me?"

Gunn says, "No," at the same time that Nathan says, "Yes."

Thomas rolls his eyes and cuddles closer to Nathan. "This reminds me of freshman year. Remember when we would put a bunch of blankets on the floor and spend all night watching movies and just, you know, talking about life."

Nathan and Gunn both smile to themselves. "Those were good times," Gunn states.

"I miss that," Nathan sighs.

"Me, too," Thomas agrees.

The three friends look at each other and smile, each of them remembering the late nights in college, the long conversations, the hangovers, and the greasy breakfasts the next morning to cure the hangovers. As they got older, their choice in alcohol got better but their ability to talk endlessly about their lives had never changed.

"Where should we start?" Thomas asks.

"You and Daniel?" Nathan suggests.

"Mmmm..." Thomas thinks about it. "No. I'll take 'What's up with Gunn's mom?' for $100."

"I wish I knew," Gunn counters.

"How about that hottie in your guest room? Is that up for discussion?"

"Next!" Nathan demands.

Thomas grimaces. "Okay. How about your dad, Nathan? Where is he?"

"Long story."

"We have all night." Thomas waits for an answer, but Gun and Nathan stay silent.

"Fine," Thomas says with a huff. He sits up and takes off his tank top, then reaches under the covers and removes his underwear. "If we're not going to talk, we're going to have sex. And I have ways of making you..."

"Fine!" Nathan laughs. "We can talk."

Thomas gives them both a huge grin before putting his head on Nathan's shoulder. "Just like old times."

Gunn mimics Thomas's pose, putting his head on Nathan's other shoulder. "Just like old times."

From there, the conversation continues deep into the night.

Chapter 18

Gunn wakes up slowly the next morning. He immediately knows he has overslept but he doesn't care. He smiles thinking of the lively and lengthy conversation with Thomas and Nathan from the night before. The three friends shared everything about their work, Thomas's relationship with Daniel, the situation with Nathan's father, the unexplained situation with Gunn's parents, and of course, Tony's sudden reappearance in Nathan's life.

It had been a long time since they had really opened up like that, and Gunn felt closer to Nathan than he had in awhile. Not just emotionally, but physically. As in, Nathan's body was pressed up against Gunn's when he woke up.

Gunn rolls onto his side to face Nathan. He kisses his fiancé's neck with a "Good morning."

Nathan stirs and opens his eyes. He glances sleepily at Gunn. "Morning." They share a kiss before Nathan rolls over onto his side to find himself face to face with Thomas.

"Hey," Nathan whispers to Thomas before giving him a friendly kiss on the cheek. "Good morning."

Thomas wrinkles his face like a little boy. "Five more minutes."

Nathan chuckles. "Fine. Five more minutes."

Thomas smiles without opening his eyes. He turns over onto his side, facing away from Nathan. Instinctively, he wraps his arms around the naked body next to him and kisses the back of his neck. "Morning."

And that body would belong to Tony, who rolls over to face Thomas. "Good morning," he says seductively as he kisses Thomas.

Thomas, still half asleep, responds, kissing Tony passionately, before he realizes what he's doing and pulls away quickly. "Tony?" he exclaims in surprise.

Nathan hears the name and looks over. "Tony?"

Gunn looks over the two men lying between him and Tony. He can only shake his head. "Unbelievable."

Tony looks at all of them with a grin.

"What are you doing, Tony?" Nathan asks, confused and a little angry. "You were not here when we fell asleep."

"I know," Tony responds, "but I woke up in the middle of the night and I heard you all talking, and I thought I'd join you. By the time I got in here, you were all sound asleep, and looking so freaking adorable. I couldn't resist."

Thomas looks under the covers at Tony. Yep, he's naked, too. "Well, good morning!" Thomas whispers to something under the covers.

"Thomas!" Nathan slaps Thomas's shoulder, and he replaces the covers.

"Just go back to your room, Tony," Gunn asks, way too politely.

Tony offers a sheepish grin. "I would, but well…" He looks under the covers. "It is morning, after all."

Gunn rolls his eyes in frustration.

"You're welcome to get out of bed first," Tony says to Gunn.

"I can't!" Gunn says with frustration.

Nathan looks at him with confusion, then understanding. He looks at Gunn under the covers. "Oh, yeah." He turns to Tony. "You don't get to see that."

"Then you go, Nathan," Tony suggests.

Nathan clears his throat. "Um, in a minute."

Tony looks at Thomas, who is still facing him, with a mischievous smile. "I can tell you're not ready to get out of bed."

Thomas shifts onto his back, and Tony does the same.

The four men stare up at the ceiling in complete silence for minutes.

Finally, Gunn can't take the silence.

"How 'bout those Packers, huh?"

And everyone looks at him like he's insane.

* * *

Across town, another Gunnunderson man wakes up with a start.

Sven rubs his beard as he looks around the room, trying to focus his eyes on the figure sitting at the end of the bed. He grabs his eyeglasses off his side table and stares at the back of Anya's head.

He leans forward and nuzzles the back of her neck.

"Good morning, Mrs. Gunnunderson."

The woman shrieks and jumps to her feet. Turns out it's Tanya, not Anya.

"Oops! Sorry, Tanya!"

"You should be sorry, mister!" She looks at Sven, then turns around in shock. "Cover yourself up, for crying in the sink!"

Sven pulls a face and pulls the sheets up to his chest. "All good."

Tanya takes a quick peek to check before turning around to face Sven again.

"What are you doing in here, Tanya?"

"Waiting for you to wake up so I can find out what the dickens you did to my sister!"

"When?" Sven asks, confused.

"I don't know!" Tanya screams. "Anya hasn't been herself since we got here, and she won't tell me why. Me! I'm her sister! She tells me everything!"

"Well, you got me," Sven confesses. "She's been like this for a week. A long week. A very long week."

Tanya sits on the bed again. "You really don't know what's wrong?"

Sven shrugs. "All I know is that I did something, or didn't do something, or forgot to do something, or forgot that I did something."

"That makes sense," Tanya sighs.

"I'm giving her some time. Sometimes that's all she needs."

"Speaking of time, you and cousin Jasper seemed to be hitting it off last night." Sven raises his eyebrows with a grin.

"How is that speaking of time?" Tanya asks.

Sven sits up and stares into space. He blinks his eyes six times in rapid succession before shaking his shoulders. "I have no idea. I was going somewhere with that though, dontcha know. And don't change the subject."

Tanya giggles quietly. "He is kinda nice, isn't he?"

"Yeah, he is," Sven agrees, playfully poking Tanya in the shoulder. "Want me to ask him if he likes you?"

Tanya blushes. "You sound like a junior high school girl." She looks down at the floor, then turns back to Sven. Now, her face is totally serious. "Would ya?"

"I'll sneak it into the conversation somehow. But now, I need a shower."

Sven stands up, momentarily forgetting that it's Tanya and not Anya in the room. He stretches his naked body as he walks to the en suite bathroom.

Tanya watches him walk away. "That reminds me. I need to trim the bushes in front of my house."

* * *

Nathan searches the refrigerator for something he can use to make breakfast for the house full of hungry men. As if breakfast could erase the memory of himself, Gunn, Thomas, and Tony all sharing a bed together. Naked. He unconsciously pulls the bathrobe he's wearing tighter around his tiny body, as if anyone could see him.

He had spent years idolizing his relationship with Tony. He figured most people did that with their first love.

No, he always corrected himself in his mind – Tony was his first crush, not his first love. That distinction was reserved for Gunn.

But since his mother had shown up for the wedding with Tony as her new assistant, Nathan had been shocked at the change in him. The confidence he had in high school had turned into arrogance. Tony's prior sexual experience had turned Nathan on at the time, but now he just seems, well, a little slutty.

Still, it's impossible for Nathan to deny the good times they had when they were younger. The clandestine meetings when Nathan's or Tony's parents were out of town. The private jokes in the high school hallway. The excitement of exploring each other's bodies like the horny teenagers they were.

But Nathan's favorite memories of that time are the conversations they had, talking about their plans for the future, discussing their frustrations with their families and friends, and imagining a time when they could spend time together as boyfriends or maybe even more.

That all changed when Nathan's father came home early from a business trip and caught the two boys in bed. He had banned Tony from the house, and Nathan's relationship with Tony withered away after that. They quickly lost touch after graduation, and Nathan rarely thought about him after that.

Yet here he was, sleeping in the guest room and coming on to him and Thomas both.

"Wait a minute," Nathan thinks to himself. "Am I jealous of Thomas? Does it bother me that Tony is interested in him?"

Nathan shakes his head at the thought.

"Screw you, Tony," he says out loud as he slams the refrigerator door closed.

Unfortunately, Tony is standing there.

"I thought you'd never ask," Tony says, wiggling his eyebrows. Nathan can't help but notice that Tony is only wearing a pair of boxer briefs that show off pretty much everything.

"Give it a rest, Tony," Nathan pleads as he averts his eyes from Tony's semi-naked body, but Tony just moves closer.

"Time is running out for one last fling before you're a married man," Tony says seductively. He slides a finger inside Nathan's robe and tries to pull it open. "No one has to know."

"I would know," Nathan replies, but he doesn't push Tony's hand away.

"Yeah, you would know," Tony counters, "and you'd remember."

Tony steps even closer and slides an entire hand inside Nathan's robe, gently rubbing his chest. "I heard Gunn in the shower, so we could be fast, like that time we snuck into the principal's office at school. Remember that?"

Nathan smiles at that memory. "We had some good times," he agrees. But then the smile disappears from his face. "And that was a long, long time ago."

Tony moves even closer, his body coming into contact with the fabric of Nathan's robe.

"How about a kiss?" he asks. "One kiss for old times' sake?"

"No, Tony," Nathan says emphatically.

As soon as the words are out of Nathan's mouth, Tony's tongue is in it, as he pushes Nathan against the refrigerator.

Just as quickly as the kiss started, it ends. Nathan shoves Tony away and wipes his mouth. Unfortunately, his robe falls open at the same time, giving Tony a view of everything. His face makes it clear that he enjoys the view.

"See?" Tony says. "Just like old times."

"Except for one thing." That statement comes from Gunn, standing at the kitchen door, his hair still damp from the shower and his bathrobe, which matches Nathan's, tied tight.

Nathan quickly closes his robe. "Gunn, it's not what you think."

"I know," Gunn states as he walks over to Nathan. "I heard." Gunn turns to face Tony. "I said there was one thing different today than in your 'old times.'"

"Which is what?" Tony asks.

"Which is that this," he puts an arm around Gunn, "is mine."

Gunn then leans down and whispers in Nathan's ear, "That sounded incredibly old-fashioned and somehow sexist, and I'm sorry."

"It also sounded kinda hot," Nathan whispers back.

"You had your kiss, and frankly, I don't blame you for wanting to kiss Nathan. I want to kiss him all day, every day." Gunn's voice gets more confident with every word. "But that kiss was your last one. I hope it will satisfy you for a very, very long time."

Tony starts to say something, but Gunn holds out a hand to stop him. "Why don't you go to your room, and for crying in the sink, put some clothes on!"

With one final glance at Nathan, Tony leaves the room.

Gunn lets out a relieved chuckle. "I can't believe that worked."

"I can." Nathan pulls Gunn toward him and kisses him. A long kiss that neither man wants to end.

When Gunn eventually pulls away, out of breath, he looks around the kitchen. "I think Thomas is in the shower," he states.

"And Tony is in his room," Nathan replies.

"We can be fast, like that time we snuck into my dad's office on campus," Gunn offers.

And in two seconds, both bathrobes hit the kitchen floor.

Chapter 19

Thomas steps into the church sanctuary and looks around with curiosity. "Why do you have to actually rehearse?"

Nathan claps a hand on his clueless friend's shoulder. "We rehearse, then we eat. Hence the term 'rehearsal dinner.'"

"I'm with you, Thomas," Gunn says from behind them. "On the day, you walk down the aisle, the guy in the funny robe asks you some questions, you kiss, then it's off to the reception. How hard can it be?"

"Pop quiz," Nathan turns to Gunn. "On which side of the preacher do you stand? Right or left?"

Gunn gazes down the aisle where the preacher waits with wedding-organizer Heather.

"I come down with my parents and go to the…" Gunn tries to remember the diagram from Heather's event binder. "My right or the preacher's right?"

Nathan turns to Thomas with a satisfied smile. "And that's why we have a rehearsal." He then grabs Gunn's arm. "Shall we practice walking down the aisle like husband and husband, spouses, groom and groom, partners for life, gay #1 and gay #2?"

"Yeah, we should probably decide on some of that verbiage."

"Ya think?" Nathan asks incredulously.

They start to walk down the aisle together, but Gunn stops.

Nathan turns and looks back at him with an inquiring shrug.

"You go ahead. I want our first time going down the aisle together to be, you know, our first time."

Thomas gasps. "You haven't walked down each other's aisles before?"

Gunn and Nathan shoot him a look, but Thomas persists.

"You haven't climbed down each other's chimneys to leave presents on Christmas morning? You haven't looked inside each other's toy sacks? You haven't cut down each other's morning Christmas trees? You haven't slid into each other's home base face first? You haven't made the beast with one muscular back and one hairy chest? You haven't..."

"Oh, my, goddess!" Gunn cries out. "Stop already."

"Fine!" Thomas reluctantly relents as the three men walk single file down the aisle of the sanctuary.

"One more," Thomas can't resist. "You've never played the priest and the altar boy?"

With that, Gunn and Nathan share a look. And then a grin.

Thomas claps his hands in feigned happiness. "Yay! I got one!"

"And I got two that night," Gunn says to himself.

The trio finally reaches the rest of the party, all huddled together in the front of the church.

Sven sits on the front pew with his parents, Gustav and Elsa. "We're not actually in the wedding party, are we?" Gustav asks. "Are we walking down the aisle or anything?"

Sven thinks about it for far longer than necessary.

"I don't think so," he comments, drawing out the statement until he decides if it's true. "No. You're not."

"Then why are we here, son?" Gustav responds with a sigh.

"We couldn't leave you all alone at home, now could we?" Sven replies.

"Yes, you could," Elsa chimes in. "We could have watched the Wheel. It's about that time, dontcha know."

Sven sighs and looks over at Jasper, who stands nearby talking with Tanya. She hangs on every word that Jasper says with an exaggerated laugh and/or hair flip.

Anya, Olivia and Heather talk with Pastor Philip Gilnacheck, a man in his 60s who seems a little confused at the events taking place today.

Other their other side, Martha stands, her cell phone to her ear, as she tries to have a heated conversation without letting anyone else know she's having a heated conversation. It's not really working.

Tony stands close to Martha, but his attention is on Nathan and Gunn making their way to the front of the church.

Heather surveys the crowd and claps her hands to get everyone's attention. "Is everyone here?"

"We're still waiting on Abby," Gunn calls out.

"Oh, yes, about that." Heather pulls a slightly panicked Gunn to the side. "Don't be alarmed. Abby is on her way, but her flight got canceled. Actually, all the flights got canceled in her area. So she's been driving all day. I talked to her about an hour ago, and she's confident she'll make it here for the ceremony tomorrow."

"Tomorrow?" Gunn whines. "I've been trying to reach her but she won't answer her phone for me."

"Like I said, Olaf, she's driving and can't pick up," Heather continued. "I got lucky and caught her while they were at a rest stop."

"And Mark and Emma? They're with her, right?"

"Of course!" Heather replies, a slightly snippy tone sneaking into her voice.

"What's wrong, Heather?" Gunn asks with real concern.

Heather shakes her head. "It's nothing."

"You two aren't fighting again, are you?"

"Don't be silly," Heather replies. "Mothers and daughters always have issues. Well, all parents and their children do, right?"

Gunn looks over at his own mom, then over to Nathan's mother, all alone. "That is true."

"But Abby will be here. She wouldn't miss this for the world. And she has a big surprise for you!"

Gunn freezes in place. "She does?"

Heather nods with satisfaction.

"She told you about it?"

"Don't be ridiculous. I asked her about it!" Heather claps her hands together in satisfaction.

"You asked her?"

"It was my idea!"

Now, Gunn looks confused. "Your idea?"

"Yes!" Heather answers smugly. "Abby is going to be our replacement soloist for *Ave Maria*!"

"Oh!" Gunn looks both surprised and relieved. "That's ... Wait, can she sing that well? It's a tough piece."

"My daughter can sing anything, and she's been practicing for two days. Plus, we can have a backup vocal track in case she messes up."

"Like Britney?"

"Like Britney. Whoever that is," Heather agrees. "Now, let's get back to the others."

Heather walks over to join the Pastor as she claps one hand against her binder.

"Yoo hoo! Everyone gather round!"

Everyone does so as they wait for instructions.

"This is Pastor Gilnacheck, and I'll be turning things over to him now. Pastor?"

Heather takes a step back and the Pastor looks around at the small crowd.

"Yes, well. Thank you, Mrs. Mancuso. I am Pastor Philip Gilnacheck, and over there…" He points to the church organ off to one side, "is our organist, Merrill Swansea, who will be providing the music for the service. Say hello, Merrill!"

The elderly gentleman stands with a creak. "Hello, Merrill!" That gets the polite laughter he expected.

Pastor Gilnacheck continues, "As you know, or at least you should, the union of two people in the holy matrimony of marriage is always a serious endeavor. In fact, I've been there every time you've embarked on this particular endeavor." He looks over at Heather with a chuckle.

Heather, however is not chuckling. "Let's move it along, Phil."

The Pastor pauses. "I have to admit, after decades in this church, this is the first one of the ceremonies I've ever done."

"Weddings?" Anya asks, shock in her voice.

"Ah. No," Pastor Gilnacheck tried to correct himself. "A same-sex wedding. With two grooms. It's all a little confusing."

"And that's why I've outlined all of the very minor changes to your text, just here," Heather hands several sheets of paper to the pastor.

Pastor Gilnacheck reads it over quickly. "Do you take this man?" He reads further. "Do you take this man? Oh, I get to ask that twice!"

Heather points to something on the page. "And at the end, you say, 'I now pronounce you husbands for life.'" She looks at Gunn and Nathan. "That's what we decided on, right?"

"That's it," Gunn nods.

"Husbands for life," Nathan agrees.

"Sounds like a prison sentence," Tony stage whispers to Nathan before noticing that Martha overheard him. "I didn't mean..."

Martha stops him with a wave of her hand. "Let's just continue, shall we?"

The pastor starts to instruct everyone but Heather takes charge. "Everyone in the wedding party, go to the back of the church."

The proper people do so, leaving Sven's parents, Jasper, Tanya, Olivia, and Tony remaining up front.

"Everyone just take a seat, somewhere other than the first two rows," Heather demands.

The Gunnundersons and the Gundersons huddle in the middle of the aisle, looking back and forth between the two sides. Olivia turns to Tanya, "What's the wedding planner's name?"

Tanya whispers back, "Anya used to call her 'box springs,' but I think it's actually Heather."

"Oh, Heather, dear," Olivia calls out.

Heather rolls her eyes. She still can't get used to the gaggle of Gunderson women. "Yes, Olivia?"

"We're a little confused as to which side we should be on," Olivia confesses.

"It doesn't matter, dear. Just sit anywhere."

"But it will matter tomorrow. We want to sit on little Olaf's side," Olivia insists as she pulls Heather closer. "I've been to enough weddings to know there's a bride's side and a groom's side, but when there are two grooms...?" She leaves the question hanging in the air.

Heather consults her binder. "Let's see. If you're facing the pulpit, Olaf's family goes on the ... left side."

Olivia and Tanya share a surprised look. "But that's the bride's –"

"It's the left side, and don't read anything into it," Heather snaps at them as she walks to the back of the church.

Olivia turns to Tanya with a raised eyebrow and guides them into their seats on the third row. Jasper joins them, sitting next to Tanya. Gustav and Elsa take the row behind them.

Tony sits, the lone person on Nathan's side of the aisle.

"Ready, Padre?" Heather calls out.

"It's just Pastor, but yes, I'm ready."

Pastor Gilnacheck nods at the organist, who begins to play.

Martha whispers in Nathan's ear, "Did you go with the traditional wedding march?"

Nathan shares a smile with Gunn. "Not exactly."

The music starts playing. A slow, slightly mournful rendition of a song that seems vaguely familiar.

"What is this song, dear?" Anya asks Gunn.

"Keep listening," Gunn advises her. "You'll figure it out."

This was something that Nathan insisted on taking over. He called in some favors and found someone to arrange one of their favorite songs for a church organ, and somehow it works.

While their family members fail to recognize the tune, a genuine laugh of recognition comes from Tony. He starts to sing along, even with the tempo slowed down for the wedding march.

"You know I'm crazy for you," Tony sings, slightly off-key. "Touch me once and you'll know it's true."

Nathan and Gunn smile in unison and turn to look at each other.

"I told you some people would get it," Nathan says with a smirk.

"And I'm glad I found something Tony Sambuco can't do – sing!" Gunn laughs.

Heather snaps her fingers. "Is everyone ready?"

The group nods in unison.

"Okay. Flower girl!"

Everyone looks around, confused.

"We don't have a flower girl," Gunn reminds her.

"I thought we were revisiting that issue," Heather says, perturbed.

"We did," Gunn says. "We decided that the role of a flower girl was demeaning to young women since it tells them that their only role in a wedding is to look pretty and to make other things look pretty."

"And your problem is…?" Heather really sounds annoyed now.

"Plus, we don't really know anyone with kids," Nathan adds.

Heather crosses something out in her binder with a sigh. "Fine. No flower girl. Best men, you're on."

Thomas steps forward, but Sven hangs back.

"I thought I was walking little Olaf down the aisle with his mother," Sven asks.

"Oh, that you remembered?" Anya asks, more than a little bitchy.

"Now, Mama," Sven tries to cool her off but she gestures him away with a wave.

"Fine," Heather concedes. "Thomas, you go first and take your position up by the pastor. Then since you're on Nathan's side, we'll have Anya and Sven escorting Gunn down. Anya, you sit with your mother. Gunn, you take your spot front and center, and Sven, you stand behind him. Then, Nathan and his parents." She looks up as soon as she realizes she made a mistake. "His mother. Sorry. Martha, you sit after you walk Nathan down the aisle, and Nathan, you come last."

Nathan starts to say something, but Gunn silences him with a point of his finger. "Don't say a word."

"And..." Heather evaluates everyone's positions, and like a racetrack umpire, cries out, "Go!"

As the music continues, the group makes their way down the aisle without any problems, unless you count Anya suddenly bursting into tears to be a problem.

The sound of Anya's sniffing causes Nathan to smile a little as he looks up at his mother. To his surprise, a few tears start to fall down her cheeks.

"Mother!" he whispers in surprise.

Martha takes a tissue that she had expertly hidden in her left hand and uses it to deftly while the tears from her face without smudging her makeup. "Did you think that woman was the only one who would be emotional at this?" Her bottom lip starts to quiver just a little bit. "My only son is getting married." She finally looks down at her son. "And I couldn't be more proud of you and the man you've become."

Nathan grasps her tighter as his eyes start to well up. "I wish Father was here."

Martha dabs her eyes again. "So do I, honey. So do I."

As Thomas takes his place near the minister, Tony winks at him, causing Thomas to blush. The Pastor catches the move and stares at Tony, shaking his head as if to say, "Don't do that again." In return, Tony winks and smiles at the Pastor, who, naturally, blushes in return.

Once Anya and Martha are both seated, Nathan takes his place in front of the minister, facing Gunn. They both smile at each other. Huge smiles of true love.

"Dearly beloved," the pastor starts, "blah blah blah. Who gives this wo- ... I mean, this man in holy matrimony?"

Nathan raises an eyebrow and shakes his head. "Yeah. We are definitely not doing that."

"Is there anything else we're not doing?" the pastor asks with confusion.

Nathan and Gunn look at each and shrug. "No. We want it traditional," Gunn replies.

"As traditional as the Supreme Court has allowed for all these many months now," Nathan adds.

The pastor pauses, thinking that over. "Right. Then let's move on, shall we? I think we all have a good sense of what happens next. I'll go through my spiel. Does anyone object? That kind of stuff."

Tony takes that moment to clear his throat. Loudly. So of course, everyone turns to look at him. He looks around with an all-too-innocent look on his face. "Sorry." He clears his throat again. "Anyone have a lozenge?"

Nathan stares daggers at Tony before turning back to the pastor. "Let's keep going."

"Good idea. Are there any readings from the Bible?"

"God, no!" Gunn and Nathan say in union.

"All righty, then!" The pastor consults his notes. "Then we have a performance of, oh! 'Ave Maria,'" he says with more than a note of surprise in his voice. "You do know that this isn't a Catholic Church, don't you?"

"That's okay," Nathan nods.

"We're not Catholic," Gunn adds.

"We really should have had pre-wedding counseling," Pastor Gilnacheck continues. "Is the soloist here?"

Heather pops her head next to the pastor's. "She'll be here tomorrow. Weather. Flight delays. You know."

"Do I?" he asks, more of himself than anyone else. He looks over at the organist. "Do you need to rehearse it?"

Merrill shakes his head. "I'm good."

"He's good," Pastor Gilnacheck confirms. "Then we have the vows. You're using standard vows?"

"No, we wrote our own," Gunn says.

"We did?" Nathan replies in mock shock.

"You better have, mister man," Gunn counters.

"Okay, we'll save those for tomorrow, I assume?" Nathan and Gunn both nod their approval. "Then, there's not much left. Blah blah blah, I now pronounce you husband and wife."

"Husbands!" Gunn and Nathan respond in unison.

"Right," Pastor Gilnacheck replies. "Husband and husband!"

Everyone in the church except for Tony cries out, "Husbands for life!"

The pastor looks surprised at the huge response. "I should write that down." He makes a note on his paper. "You may kiss the ... whatever."

Gunn and Nathan lean in to kiss but the pastor stops them. "Not now! It's bad luck!" He sighs. "Then you turn to face the congregation, and you walk back down the aisle. Any questions?"

There's a long silence, finally punctuated by Tony's voice. "Where's the bar?"

Chapter 20

As an homage to their favorite Christmas movie, *A Christmas Story*, Nathan and Gunn had decided to hold the rehearsal dinner at their favorite Chinese food restaurant. Absolutely no one got the reference.

The collection of Nathan's and Gunn's families and friends sits at a large round table that's a little too big for their wedding party since no one had bothered to change the reservation. Empty chairs remind everyone of the absence of Nathan's father, Abby and her clan, and the no-show soloist and her plus one.

Despite the missing loved ones, everyone agrees on one way to make the rehearsal dinner be as fun as possible.

"Two glasses of Malbec here," Nathan calls out to the waiter hovering besides the table, as he gestures to himself and Gunn.

"Champagne, please," Martha demands politely.

"Bourbon, neat," requests Tony.

"Two ... no, three pitchers of beer for us," Sven says to the waiter.

"And I'll have a cosmopolitan," Thomas says as he closes his menu with satisfaction.

Everyone stares at the waiter, who hasn't written down any of their drink orders. There's a slight whiff of panic in his eyes.

The waiter hesitates and takes a deep breath before speaking. "I am so sorry for the inconvenience, but we are not serving alcohol at this time."

A stunned silence washes over the table.

Gunn finally leans over and whispers to Nathan, "Did he just say what I think he just said?"

Nathan nods and then addresses the waiter. "We come in here once a week, and we always have drinks with our meal."

Martha speaks to her son with real concern. "Once a week? Nathan, what have I told you about the dangers of MSG?"

"No MSG!" the waiter yells. "And no alcohol!" He looks at Nathan. "There was a slight problem with the paperwork for our liquor license, but it should all be fixed by the next time you come in."

The waiter pulls out his ordering pad and addresses the table. "Can I interest anyone in some refreshing iced tea?"

* * *

Twenty minutes later, huge platters of Chinese food are being placed on the large lazy Susan in the middle of the table. Beef with broccoli, sweet and sour pork, spicy tofu with vegetables, General Tso's chicken, drunken noodles, fried and steamed rice, and more fill the space between everyone's half-empty glasses of iced tea. There's enough food for an army, but the Hunan Palace and Garden has never met the combined eating power of the Gunnunderson and Gunderson families.

Jasper makes sure that Sven's parents have enough to eat before piling a huge selection of meats on his own plate. Tanya points out all of Olivia's favorite dishes and serves them both.

Anya covers her plate with steamed white rice, then covers half of it with sweet and sour pork, and the other half with Kung Pao chicken. Everything then gets covered in a layer of lo mein.

"Got enough food there, Mama?" Sven playfully asks.

"So I'm getting fat?" Anya asks as she shoves a forkful of her Chinese concoction into her mouth. "Is that what you're saying?"

"No! That's not what I said!" Sven cries out before pausing and staring into space. "Is it?" he wonders aloud. He blinks as he thinks back over his comment. Finally, he shrugs in resignation as Anya turns her back to him and continues eating.

A few chairs down, Martha selects a single spoonful of the otherwise-ignored spicy tofu before sliding it to Nathan, who puts some on his plate in solidarity with his mother.

Nathan offers the platter to Gunn. "Want some?"

Gunn wrinkles his nose. "Yeah. No." He looks around the table before whispering to Nathan. "Are we supposed to say something? Make a toast?"

"A toast?" Nathan replies sarcastically. "With what?"

Gunn rolls his eyes, picks up his glass, and stands. "Can I have everyone's attention, please?"

"I guess we're making a toast, after all," Nathan says under his breath as he grabs his glass and stands to join Gunn.

"Nathan and I want to thank you all for coming," Gunn starts out, immediately drawing a round of applause from the guests. "I honestly never thought we'd be here, not because I didn't want it but because I didn't think it would ever be legally possible. But here we are, thanks to the work of people like Nathan."

That gets another round of applause, as Nathan feigns embarrassment and gives just the slightest bow to the table.

"If I haven't done it before, I want to publicly thank Nathan for what he's done to ensure marriage equality, and more importantly, I want to thank him for what he's done in granting me marriage equality." Gunn raises his glass to Nathan. "Thank you for marrying me."

The two men clink glasses and then give each other a sweet, loving kiss.

"Get a room!" Thomas yells out playfully.

As the group laughs, Gustav slowly gets to his feet. As everyone notices him, Gunn and Nathan take a seat, and everyone turns their attention to Gustav.

"I don't know if it's my turn to speak, but I'm old, and ..." He pauses, thinking of another reason, and coming up short. "That's it. I'm old, so I'm going to speak."

He looks directly at Gunn. "We've never really talked about it, but I have known many men like you in my lifetime. Men I've worked with. Men I've gone to church with. Men that I have been proud to call my friends. And they all had one thing in common."

His wife Elsa interrupts his speech. "They were all in love with you, Gustav!"

That makes everyone at the table laugh, including Gustav.

"That's probably true, and who can blame them," Gustav jokes. But then, his voice takes on a serious tone. "No, what they all had in common was the fact that they had to hide who they were and who they loved. In fact, most of them were too scared to love someone, anyone, they way that my grandson here loves his fiancé.

"I am so happy that our little Olaf doesn't have to hide in the shadows and deny who he is." Gustav stares into Gunn's eyes as tears start to form in his own. "I am so proud of you, Olaf, and I hope that you and Nathan have as good of a life together, and as many years together, as your grandmother and I have."

Gunn stands, walks over to his grandfather, and the two men exchange a long, warm hug. Gunn tries to think of something to say, but their embrace says it all.

* * *

The rest of the rehearsal dinner passed without incident, filled with casual conversation and many stories about Gunn's childhood. Martha joined in as much as possible, and it was obvious, even to her, that she didn't know as much about her son as the Gunnundersons did about theirs.

In addition, Martha kept excusing herself, going outside, and taking phone calls that never seemed to be filled with good news.

Gunn's only concern was the tension between his parents.

"You still don't know what's bothering Mom?" Gunn asks his father when Anya had left the table to visit the restaurant's bathroom.

"I am clueless, son," Sven replies.

"I know that, but what about Mom?"

Sven stares at his son, not getting the joke.

"I don't get it," he finally responds.

Gunn puts a comforting hand on Sven's shoulder. "Just try to figure it out and make sure she's in a good mood for the wedding tomorrow."

"I'll do my best," Sven answers, sliding his hands inside his pants pockets. As he does so, he notices something hiding in his right pocket. He pulls his hand out, holding a tightly rolled joint.

He offers it to Gunn. "Hey, you guys want this for your bachelor party?"

"Dad!" Gunn cries out in shock. He quickly takes the joint from his father before anyone else sees it. "How many times have I told you not to pull these out in public?"

Sven thinks about it. "I have no idea."

"Okay," Gunn responds with a sigh. "How many times has the dean asked you not to pull these things out in public? As in, not in class?"

"Once or twice, I think."

Gunn shoves the joint inside his jacket pocket. "And there's no bachelor party."

Sven looks confused. "Really? That Tony guy told me we were all going out after dinner."

Gunn takes a deep sigh and looks over at Tony. "And where exactly did he say we were going?"

Chapter 21

Two hours later, Gunn has his answer in the form of the tassels spinning from the silicone-filled breasts of Candi, the lead dancer at Strip Search, the most well-known "exotic dancing" club in town. Not that Gunn had ever been there, but he had heard plenty of his straight students talking about it.

Gunn and Nathan sit at a table in the back of the club, as far away from the action as possible. They sip twenty-dollar cocktails and watch the strippers with bemusement.

"Do you think she's handsomely paid?" Nathan says with a fake British accent.

"I think that quoting *Breakfast at Tiffany's* isn't going to make this evening any more enjoyable," Gunn responds.

"Oh, come on," Nathan says, poking Gunn in the shoulder. "This is fascinating and you know it. And they aren't allowed to take off their g-strings, so we aren't in danger of seeing ... that stuff down there."

"What stuff?"

Nathan stares at him with a "you know what I mean" grimace.

"Oh!" Gunn exclaims. "Their vaginas!"

"Yes," Nathan agrees. "That stuff."

The men watch Candi's incredibly nuanced on-stage interpretation of the song *Cherry Pie* before Gunn adds, "I think

I'd rather see her vagina than her tattoo that says 'Daddy Loves Me' that's right next to her vagina."

"She's a psychology case study ready for publication," Nathan responds. "All she needs is –"

"Chicken wings!" Thomas exclaims, interrupting Nathan's train of thought. He sits next to Nathan and sets an overflowing plate of wings on the table, the sauce dripping generously onto the surface. "You guys should really check out the buffet. And it's free!"

"Yes, if you don't count the forty-dollar cover charge, it's totally free," Gunn nods.

"Exactly!" Thomas replies before grabbing a messy wing and shoving it into his mouth. "Where's Tony?" he asks through a mouthful of meat.

Gunn points toward the stage. "Up front, with my dad."

Sure enough, Tony and Sven sit right by the stage. Tony waves a five-dollar bill at Candi, who staggers over to let him slip it into her g-string.

"Thank you, I'm sure," Candi says with a smile. She turns her gaze to Sven, who isn't paying attention at all, thanks to the smoke he and Tony shared in the club's parking lot before coming in. Luckily, strip club parking lots are one of the places where you can light up without caring what anyone thinks.

But while Sven isn't watching Candi, she stares at him intently as she gyrates her tassels before a metaphorical light bulb goes off over her head.

"Professor Gunnunderson!" she cries out with glee.

Startled, Sven looks up in surprise. He pulls the glasses from atop his head, puts them on, and looks at Candi – her face, not anything else.

"Candice Fallmeyer!" he finally exclaims with the snap of his fingers.

Candi never stops dancing as she converses with Sven. "It's so good to see you, Professor Gunnunderson."

"Oh, yeah, you betcha," Sven replies, nodding his head, not sure what to say to the almost-naked woman spreading her legs in front of him. "Well, what have you been up to, for crying in the sink?"

Candi goes down in the splits and leans her head toward Sven. "Oh, this and that. I'm almost done with my degree."

"In dancing?" Sven asks.

Candi laughs. "No, silly! I'm getting my MBA in marketing. Oh! And I have a blog with videos and a webcam and everything! You should check it out!"

As the song ends, Candi turns to Sven with a pout. "Time to go."

"Well, it was good seeing you, Candace." Sven awkwardly looks in his wallet and pulls out a ten. He holds it out for Candi, who gestures toward her g-string. Sven's eyes bulge out in panic. He finally hands the bill to Tony. "Um, can you take care of this?"

Sven stands and leaves as Tony slips the bill to Candi. "I think you're deeply and profoundly talented," he whispers to her.

Sven joins Gunn, Nathan, and Thomas at their table. "She was one of my students!" he exclaims, gesturing to the now-empty stage.

"You must be so proud," Gunn replies.

"She said she has a webcam," Sven says. "You think it's one of those sites where she shows you how to make, like, low-fat dinners? Oh, your mom loves those sites."

The younger men pause and stare at each other. It's a full minute before Gunn finally speaks. "You know, it's probably best that we not tell mom that you knew the stripper at my bachelor party."

Sven shrugs.

"It's a shame Granddad and Jasper couldn't join us," Gunn says to his father.

"Hey, I offered," Sven says as if it was the craziest thing in the world for his father to decline. He spots Thomas's plate. "Ooh! Chicken wings!"

He heads off to the buffet just as Tony joins them and takes a seat.

"There couldn't at least be a hot policeman who comes in and threatens to arrest us before pulling off his uniform?" Gunn asks of Tony.

Tony grins at him, a mischievous grin. "I can always strip for you boys when we get home."

"Yes, please!" Thomas replies with a wag of his eyebrows.

"No, please!" Gunn counters. "A, we're not boys, and B, it's not your home. It's our home. Me and Nathan."

Gunn puts a protective arm around Nathan's shoulders.

Nathan smiles and leans over to whisper in Gunn's ear. "But we do have that police uniform in our costume closet."

"Ssshhh!" Gunn replies. "That's for my birthday."

Chapter 22

Gunn wakes up the next morning with a smile, knowing that this is his wedding day. He rolls over to give Nathan a kiss, but the bed is empty.

He throws on some sweats and makes his way to the kitchen, where he finds Nathan making scrambled eggs, bacon, and bagels. "I'm going to expect this every morning once we're married."

"Yeah, you just keep expecting that," Nathan says as he reaches into the refrigerator and pulls out a carton of orange juice and a bottle of champagne. "Mimosas?"

"Does that set the right tone to start our marriage with alcohol?" Gunn asks.

"Mimosas aren't alcohol," Nathan responds. "They're a healthy combination of orange juice and grape juice. I'm surprised they're not on every diet."

He grabs two champagne glasses, tosses in a splash of orange juice in each one, pops open the bubbly with a flourish, fills each glass to the top, and hands one to Gunn.

"To the next fifty years together."

"Is that when I get to trade you in for a new model?"

"Deal."

They clink the glasses together in a toast.

* * *

At Sven and Anya's house, Heather is the first to arrive, carrying her massive wedding-planner binder in one hand and a garment bag containing her dress in the other.

Anya greets her in the kitchen with barely a word. She pours Heather a cup of coffee, slides it across the kitchen island, and wipes tears from her eyes.

"Good lord, Anya. Are you crying again?" Heather has no time for pleasantries this morning. "He's your son. He's getting married. There's no need to carry on like this."

Anya grabs a kitchen towel and loudly blows her nose. "Everything's about to change, Heather. I'm too old for change."

Heather sighs and rolls her eyes dramatically. "I can't believe I'm about to say this, but you're not that old, Anya. And you've adapted to changes in your life better than just about anyone I know."

Anya sniffles. "Really?"

"Absolutely," Heather replies with a nod. "The way you handled Olaf's coming out. Starting a catering business with me, of all people."

"Oh, yeah, well, that was a real challenge, dontcha know!" Anya giggles through her tears.

"And the way you deal with Sven being … well, Sven being Sven."

That makes Anya start crying even harder. Heather comes closer and puts an arm around Anya's shoulder.

"And I didn't know you back then, but the way you dealt with having a baby right out of high school? Judging by how Olaf turned out, it's clear you handled that well, too. You're a good mother, Anya Gunderson Gunnunderson. And you're a good friend. But more importantly…"

She pauses and looks Anya square in the eyes.

"You'd better be a good baker, because I need to see the wedding cake."

That makes Anya smile. "It's in the fridge," Anya whispers. "I'll assemble the layers at the reception."

Heather moves to the refrigerator, opens the door, and peers inside.

A huge smile spreads across her face.

"Oh, Anya! They're perfect!"

* * *

"Oh, Anya! They're awful!"

Sven stands in front of a full-length mirror in his and Anya's bedroom. He evaluates his appearance with a frown.

He's wearing nothing but a pair of tighty-whitey briefs.

"Why does the woman insist I wear underwear to the wedding?" he says to his reflection.

"Because the tux is rented and you never know whose junk has been in there before you," his father answers from the doorway. Gustav is already dressed for the wedding in a nice, conservative gray suit. His light blue tie provides a vibrant pop of color against the crisp white shirt.

Sven waves his hands in a dismissive gesture. "Pish, posh, Papa. Plus, I've already tried the pants on."

"And think of how many men have done that before you," Gustav counters.

That makes Sven stop and think. "Underwear it is."

* * *

In her hotel suite, Martha looks at her glorious red hair in the bathroom mirror, making last-minute adjustments here and there. She wants to look perfect.

There's really only one thing she wants, however, and it has nothing to do with her appearance.

She picks up her cell phone from the bathroom counter and checks it for the hundredth time this morning. No calls.

"Oh, Peter. What is going on?"

Martha makes her way into the living room, grabbing her purse along the way. She spies an envelope on the coffee table with "Nathan and Olaf" written in big letters across its front. She picks up the envelope and stares at it, sighing.

She thinks back to an argument she and Nathan had shortly after his college graduation. As usual, she and Peter had given him a generous check for his present, as they had done for every birthday, every Christmas, and every special occasion in the past.

This time, Nathan took the envelope with a shrug. "Why do you do this?" he had asked.

"What do you mean, darling?"

"I mean, I appreciate the checks. I really do. But they're so … impersonal. You give someone a check when you don't really know them. Or don't like them."

"Nathan! Really!"

"I thought we were getting along so much better now."

That was true. Since Nathan had insisted on bringing Gunn into his life with his parents, they had warmed to Gunn and to their own son, as well.

"I think we are," Martha had countered.

"Then don't give me a check for graduation. Give me something that I want. Or better yet, give me something that you want me to have."

"Like what?"

Nathan had laughed. "I can't tell you, Mother. That's for you to decide. If you have to give me something – and frankly, you don't – give me something from the heart."

Those words echo in Martha's ears this morning.

"Something from the heart, huh?"

She picks up her cell phone and dials.

"It's Martha Stanford. I need you to do something for me. Today."

***

As the Gunnundersons and Gundersons meet at Sven and Anya's house before heading to the church together, Olivia pulls Anya aside.

"Gosh, I sure do wish your dad was here today," Olivia says to her daughter.

"That's so funny!" Anya exclaims. "I've been thinking about him, too. Golly, I see so much of him in little Olaf."

"Except for the whole gay thing, dontcha know."

That prompts a loud round of giggles between the two women.

"Oh!" Olivia looks around to make sure no one is listening. "I got the boys matching foam cheeseheads. They're all wrapped up in the car. You don't think anyone else had the same idea, do ya?"

"Geez, that's a super fantastic idea!" Anya says. "They're gonna love 'em."

(Naturally, Anya had had the same idea. As did Tanya. And Jasper. And even Thomas. In the end, Gunn and Nathan received a dozen cheeseheads – and they cherished every one.)

* * *

After pushing aside a mound of wedding presents, Nathan and Gunn eat their breakfast at their seldomly used dining table.

"Have you seen Thomas this morning?" Nathan asks Gunn, who gestures to the couch.

"His blankets and stuff are still there. Must be in the shower."

"I don't hear the water running."

"Ssshhh!" Gunn whispers. "Do you hear that?"

A low and frequent bang echoes in the walls.

"What is that?" Nathan asks.

The bang gets louder but the guys can't tell where it's coming from.

"Is it upstairs?" Gunn wonders.

Soon, it becomes clear that the sound is indeed coming from upstairs. From the guest room, in fact. Because the banging is soon accompanied by the sound of Tony's voice.

"Yes," Tony's voice cuts through the walls, getting louder. "Yes! Yes! Oh, Nathan, yes!"

And just as quickly as it had started, the banging ends.

Gunn stares at Nathan with a bemused smile. "Now that's what I call an extremely long dick."

Nathan shakes a finger at his fiancé. "You do not get to quote *Peter's Friends* to me at this moment."

"Oh, come on!" Gunn pleads. "When am I ever going to get to use that line again?"

Before Nathan can answer, Thomas comes plodding down the stairs, a sheet wrapped around his otherwise naked body.

He stops dramatically at the bottom of the stairs. "My therapist is going to have a field day with this one."

Nathan and Gunn try not to laugh, but they can't help it, especially when Tony follows Thomas down the stairs.

"Come on, it happens to everyone," Tony claims.

"Tony?" Nathan calls out to his former flame.

Tony sees Nathan and Gunn at the table and rolls his eyes. "Yes?"

"I think it would be a good idea if you did <u>not</u> come to the wedding today."

"And maybe you should be gone by the time we get back?" Gunn suggests.

Nathan nods in agreement. "Good idea."

Tony has no response. He just starts back up the stairs with a sigh.

"Hey, Tony?" Nathan says.

Tony stops and turns around. "What?"

"Good luck."

Chapter 23

Gunn stands at the back of the sanctuary, carefully pushing the doors open just enough to let him stare at the people who have come to see him and Nathan get married.

Family members. Friends. A few professors from the university. Some of their students. Even some people he doesn't recognize as the adrenaline courses through his veins.

Suddenly, a hand takes Gunn's hand.

"Ready?"

Nathan stands beside him. Gunn didn't even hear him walk up.

"Is it wrong to be nervous?" Gunn asks.

Nathan lets out a deep breath. "I thought it was just me."

"I got something to calm you down," Sven's voice whispers in Gunn's ear.

"Sven!" Anya cries out in disbelief.

Sven pats his jacket pocket and wags his eyebrows at his son. "If you need it..."

"Do you have the rings in there, too, Dad?"

Panicked, Sven reaches inside his pocket and feels around. With a sigh of relief, he pulls out a small box that clearly contains the rings.

Nathan whistles as his mother enters the room. "Mother, you look so beautiful."

Martha tilts her head to one side. "I know," she says playfully before caressing Nathan's right cheek with her left hand. "I love you, Nathan. I'm sorry that–"

Nathan interrupts her. He doesn't want to hear anything negative on this day. "I love you, too."

Heather pushes Thomas to the front of the group, closest to the door leading to the sanctuary. "You're first down the aisle. Do you remember where to go?"

Thomas nods. "Under the huppa."

Heather stares at him for a long time. Finally, she says, "You're kidding, right?"

"I'm kidding."

Heather sighs. "This is not the day for that." She clears her throat to get everyone's attention. "Are we ready?"

The group looks to Gunn and Nathan, waiting.

Gunn turns to Nathan. "I can do this."

Nathan smiles. "Then let's do this."

Chapter 24

"Dearly beloved, we are gathered here today to witness the marriage of Nathan Hamish Stanford and Olaf Erick Gunnunderson." The pastor's words fill the sanctuary and cause Nathan and Gunn to smile sweetly at each other.

In fact, everyone is smiling sweetly as the ceremony begins – except maybe for Anya, who can't manage to smile through her tears, even as she pulls tissue after tissue from the sleeve of her beautiful dress.

Gunn can hear the pastor speaking but he can't really understand the words as his mind thinks back over his life with Nathan.

Their first all-too-naked meeting in their dorm room, freshman year.

The time spent during their college years, before Gunn had come out to his parents, when the campus was the only place where he felt like he could be himself.

The fateful Christmas vacation when Nathan had surprised him by showing up at Gunn's parents' house, sparking a chain of events that ended with Gunn coming out at Christmas dinner.

The year after college when Gunn had gone to teach overseas, when it seemed that their affection for each other was all they needed to survive.

The time spent together in Manhattan, sharing an apartment with Thomas.

The time apart when the boys became men and their jobs took them to different parts of the country as they figured out who they wanted to be and what they wanted to do.

The last few months living together, teaching at the same university, and building a real home together.

And of course, sitting together, waiting on the Supreme Court marriage equality ruling, and celebrating the only way possible – by proposing to each other.

All of that led to today. Their wedding day.

Gunn knows that his love for Nathan will never change, yet he also realizes the significance of the ceremony itself. He knows that, despite its symbolism, marriage is largely a legal transition, joining two people in a union that is recognized – legally recognized – by the rest of the world.

But it's the symbolism that matters to Gunn today. He thinks of the thrill he felt when he and Nathan picked up their marriage license, buoyed by the congratulations of complete strangers who acknowledged the importance of the act.

He thinks of the rings he purchased in Spain so many years ago, when the thought of proposing to Nathan was going to mean a "commitment ceremony" and not an actual marriage. Even after their engagement, they kept the rings hidden, sacred, until today.

Yes, he also thinks briefly of the Waterford vase and the Crate & Barrel plates and the four-slice stainless steel toaster they had received as gifts. But not because they had wanted or needed the gifts, but because not so long ago he would have thought it impossible that his grandparents and his parents' friends and even Nathan's parents' friends would have supported a "gay wedding."

He thinks of Nathan's parents and the way they had slowly warmed up to him after taking so many years to truly accept their son's sexuality. He looks out on the crowd and sees Martha's smiling face, and he wishes that Peter was here with them, as well.

His eyes move to his mother in her seat, then to his father standing beside him as his best man, and he remembers their acceptance of his coming out that Christmas, the way they welcomed Nathan with open arms, and their willingness to stand up for their son's happiness. But most of all, he remembers their unwavering love for him.

Gunn wipes away a tear before it can make its way down his cheek, as he looks at Nathan and finally lets the pastor's words come back into his ears.

"If there is anyone present who has just cause why these two people should not be lawfully married, speak now or forever hold your peace."

For some reason, Gunn holds his breath after this part of the ceremony. Waiting. And then …

Nothing happens.

Gunn smiles at Nathan and raises his eyebrows in relief.

"Wait!"

Gunn and Nathan turn their heads in unison, almost in slow motion, as the doors at the back of the sanctuary fly open behind the powerful voice, but the light from the alcove beyond makes it hard to identify the figure slamming the doors against their hinges.

Now, everyone turns to see the source of the loud cry.

Chapter 25

As the doors spring back to their closed position, the figure of Peter Stanford steps into the sanctuary.

"Am I too late?" he asks as he slicks back his hair with his hands.

"Dad?" Nathan cries out in surprise.

"Peter?" Martha stands, the confusion on her face quickly turning to elation. "Peter!"

Martha steps into the aisle and walks quickly back to meet her husband with a warm hug.

At the same time, Nathan turns to go to his parents, but he stops himself and turns to the pastor first. "I'll be right back," he says before starting to rush to his parents.

Halfway down the aisle, Nathan stops abruptly, a panicked look on his face. He turns around, goes back to the front of the church, and puts a hand on Gunn's face.

"I'll be right back," he says with a wink before going back to find his father.

Gunn looks bashfully at the pastor. "I'll just wait here." The pastor nods in confused agreement.

At the back of the sanctuary, Nathan meets his parents, and his father pulls him close in a tight embrace.

"I am so, so sorry, son," Peter whispers in Nathan's ear.

"What happened?" Nathan asks as soon as he pulls away.

Sensing everyone's eyes and ears on them, Peter pulls his wife and son into the entryway to explain.

"Tell us everything, Peter," Martha implores.

"Wait," Nathan interjects. "Did you break out of jail?"

Peter laughs and hugs his son again. "Nathan, I love that you think I'd be capable of breaking out of jail. It's actually far simpler and much more complicated than that."

"Your attorneys wouldn't tell me anything or let me speak to you," Martha says. "I've called and called. I've been worried sick, Peter Stanford!"

"I know, I know," Peter sighs. "And the news stories were partly true. The government is investigating my company, my bosses in particular. What they didn't report, what they didn't know, is that ..." He pauses dramatically. "I've been helping them out."

"What do you mean?" Martha asks.

"Oh, my goddess," Nathan exclaims. "Are you a spy?"

Martha's eyes go wide at that accusation, but Peter shuts his eyes and nods in agreement.

"It's a long story," Peter says.

"Well, we only have the church for the next hour," Nathan replies, his comments dripping with sarcasm.

And so Peter tells them an abbreviated version of how he had been approached by government officials over a year ago, asking for – no, demanding – his help in finding information on his superiors who were suspected of a variety of crimes, specifically tax evasion, which had been Peter's area of expertise in terms of finding the documentation the government needed.

Nathan stands quietly while Martha quickly asks a slew of questions that take Nathan completely by surprise. He realizes how little he knows about his father's business and the marital issues his parents had been facing over the past year because of his father's activities. Nathan sighs with relief when his father explains that he was forced to keep the investigation secret, even from Martha, and that his arrest was part of a bigger scheme to keep his bosses in the dark.

After sharing his tale as best he could, Peter checks his watch. "Nathan, don't you have someplace you need to be?"

"Probably." Nathan smiles at his father. "I'm so glad you're here."

"Me, too," Martha agrees, giving her husband a quick kiss on the cheek.

"We can slip in quietly, if you want," Peter suggests.

That only makes Nathan laugh. "After that entrance, not a chance!"

The Stanford trio enter the sanctuary together, quickly seeing that everyone is still turned to face them.

Nathan clears his throat. "As you were." He gestures for everyone to turn around, which they do.

He then shares a big smile with his husband-to-be before addressing the pastor. "If you don't mind, we're going to do this bit again."

And with that, Nathan pulls his mother on his left side, intertwining their arms so they can walk down the aisle again. But then he pulls his father to his right side and joins their arms.

With a satisfied smile, Nathan walks down the aisle to his betrothed, accompanied by both of his parents.

When they arrive at the front of the church, Nathan gives his mother a quick kiss and gives his father a hug before once again joining Gunn at the altar.

Martha moves to the right to take her previous seat, but Peter moves to the left, causing them to bump into each other in the middle of the aisle.

"We're on this side, dear," Martha whispers, quickly guiding Peter to their pew.

Once they're seated, Peter looks around, a little confused. He leans over and whispers to Martha. "But this is …" He stops himself before finishing his thought.

"This is what?" Martha responds quietly.

"You know," Peter states with confidence.

"No, I don't know," Martha says, a little exasperated.

Peter rolls his eyes. "This is the groom's side."

"Yes," Martha replies. "Yes, it is."

"Does that mean ... ?" He lets the question hang in the air.

Martha turns to him with a smile and nods. "Apparently so."

Peter mulls that for a moment. "Huh" is his only response.

Martha leans in to whisper in his ear again. "Aren't you forgetting something, dear?"

Their eyes lock and a satisfied smile crosses Martha's face.

Peter reaches into his jacket pocket, pulls out his wallet, and reaches inside.

He removes a one-hundred-dollar bill, which he slowly hands to Martha.

"I told you so," Martha whispers.

Peter returns his wallet to his jacket pocket as he looks at his son. The corners of his mouth turn slightly upward as he says softly, "That's my boy."

Meanwhile, the pastor tries to get the ceremony back on track as Nathan takes his position again, but not before leaning close to Gunn. "Everything's okay. I'll tell you all about it later."

"You do that," Gunn responds.

The pastor consults his notes. "Let's see, where were we? Oh, yes!" He clears his throat and address the crowd once again, authority in his voice.

"If there is anyone present who has just cause why these two people should not be lawfully married, speak now or forever hold your peace."

Gunn and Nathan look around the church, eyes narrowed as if daring anyone to make a sound.

No one does.

Well, until the back doors fly open once again as a voice screams out, "Oh, hell no!"

Chapter 26

The guests look back, startled, and they start talking to each other, many of them wondering who had the nerve to stop this wedding. Again.

But some of them recognize the voice immediately. One of those people is Heather, who stands and claps her hands together in joy.

"Abby! You made it!"

Sure enough, the owner of the voice, the person who slammed the church doors open, is none other than Abby Mancuso, Heather's daughter and Gunn's close friend since childhood.

Abby strikes a pose inside the sanctuary, her phenomenal head of curly hair continuing to move of its own accord.

"Were you bitches seriously going to get married without me?" she cries out, pointing her fingers at Gunn and Nathan, who look at each other, extremely relieved that this was the person interrupting the ceremony for the second time.

Abby marches down the aisle toward the waiting couple, loving the fact that all eyes are now on her. She wears a fabulous hippie-chic tan dress and knee-length faux-leather boots, looking like she just stepped off the cover of *Hemp Monthly*.

But she's not alone.

Following close on Abby's heels is a tall, bald African-American man in an impeccably tailored forest-green suit, and a stunning Hispanic woman in a maroon dress that flawlessly shows off every one of her curves.

Heather moves past the people in her row in order to meet her daughter in the aisle.

"You look fabulous, darling," Heather declares as she and Abby exchange air kisses.

"I know," Abby responds as she checks out Heather's dress. "And you look ... were you going for matronly?"

Heather snarls at her, but soon the snarl turns into a smile. "It's so good to have you home."

Abby gestures to her companions. "You remember my boyfriend, Mark, and my girlfriend, Emma." She makes it a statement, not a question.

"Of course!" Air kisses all around. "So glad you could both make it. Now, have a seat."

Heather gestures where Mark and Emma should sit, and they accommodate her. Heather then pulls Abby close. "Are you ready for your song?"

"I am so ready," Abby responds, "but there's something I need to discuss with the boys first."

Abby crooks her index finger, demanding that Gunn and Nathan join her for a discussion. The guys chuckle and turn to the pastor. "We'll be right back," they say in unison.

As Abby, Gunn, and Nathan move to a corner of the sanctuary to talk, Heather stands next to the pastor and addresses the crowd.

"I'm sure they won't be a minute," she says with way too much confidence.

"Are all gay weddings like this?" Pastor Gilnacheck quietly asks Heather.

Heather turns her head to face him. "It's not a gay wedding," she snaps, a bit of the old Heather coming out. "It's just a wedding! Or it will be if it ever …"

But before she can finish, Gunn's voice echoes in the church.

"Are you serious?" he cries out. But he's not surprised or angry. He's happy. "Are you serious?" he repeats, a huge smile on his face.

Abby nods her head and jumps up and down as she hugs both Gunn and Nathan. Then, she steps back to watch the two men hug each other.

"She's serious," Gunn declares to Nathan.

"I heard," Nathan responds with a grin.

"We're …" Gunn can't finish the thought.

"We are!" Nathan agrees.

"Actually, I am," Abby interjects.

The three of them embrace again.

Finally, Heather can't take it anymore. "What's going on with you three? You're what, Abby?"

Abby looks at Gunn and Nathan with a nervous grin on her face, her eyebrows raised in an unasked question.

The men look at each other and shrug, then back to Abby with a nod.

And with that, Abby turns to the crowd and yells out, "I'm pregnant!"

"What?" Heather cries.

Now it's Gunn's turn to yell out. "With our baby!"

With that, Anya jumps to her feet, her face filled with questions. "What?" is all she can manage.

"We're having a baby!" Nathan says, looking over at his parents.

Martha stands as she clasps her hands together in what can only be described as joy. "What?"

"I'm just the surrogate," Abby declares.

"What?" Heather asks, remembering the time Abby served as a surrogate for friends of hers a few years ago.

"Oh, yeah. She's just the surrogate," Nathan says, as if it were obvious. "Was that not clear?"

And with a single voice, the entire wedding crowd says in unison, "What?"

Gunn and Nathan make their way back to their positions with the pastor. "We didn't want to say anything until we knew for sure," Gunn says, looking at his parents. "We did the procedure a couple of months ago, close to Abby's home so she wouldn't have to travel."

Sven puts a hand on Gunn's shoulder and snaps his fingers. "That trip you two took to North Carolina?"

Gunn nods.

"Oh, that you remember?" Anya yells at Sven.

"Oh, Mama, why are you so angry? Our little boy's gonna have a baby." With that, Sven gives Gunn a warm hug.

Anya's lower lip starts to quiver. "But he can't have a baby!" She cries out as she starts to cry.

"For goodness sakes, why not?" Sven asks.

"Because!" Anya says between tears. Finally, she just says it. "Because I'm having a baby!"

The entire sanctuary goes silent, finally broken by an outburst by Heather.

"What the fuck?"

Sven's eyes go wide in shock. He's unable to say a word.

Gunn, however, looks surprised but pleasantly so. "You're having a …?" Gunn asks.

Anya nods as she pulls tissues from her sleeve and blows her nose. "A baaaaaaaaaaaaaaaaaby!" she exclaims.

"Is that why you've been so mad at me?" Sven asks, a little confused. Well, more confused than usual.

"You idiot!" Anya slaps his arm. "I'm mad because I told you a week ago and you forgot!"

The church goes silent again as everyone stares at Sven.

Sven, meanwhile, stares into space. "That does sound like something I would do."

Gunn turns to the pastor and says, "I'll be right back," and then points at Nathan, saying, "That goes for you, too," before he steps away to go to his parents.

"Mom, tell me what happened."

Anya wipes her nose. "We were in the living room, putting up Christmas decorations. You know how that always puts your dad in a good mood. And he was watching that cartoon special he likes. You know the one?"

Gunn nods. "The materialistic beagle."

That makes Sven chuckle. "That's a good one."

"You hush up, Sven," Anya demands before turning back to Gunn. "And I told him. I was so nervous. I'm too old to be a mom again. But I told him, and he put his arm around me, and said, 'That's good, isn't it, Mama?' That's what he said. And then he went down to his basement, and he never said another word about it. Whenever I tried to bring it up and talk about it, he wouldn't discuss it."

Now, Anya turns to face Sven. "That's when I figured out that you were as high as a kite, and that you had completely forgotten what I told you, and then I thought, I can't raise another kid at my age with a father like him." She gestures angrily to Sven. "What if it has two heads? Or a tail?"

"What if it turns out gay?" Gunn asks.

"What?" Anya responds. "You know I wouldn't care about that."

"Well, that's what you got the first time around, and Dad certainly hasn't changed since then. Why would anything be different this time?"

Anya sniffs and wipes the tears from her eyes. "I guess you're right."

"Wait a second." Sven rolls his eyes around in his head, trying to remember something. For once, he actually is remembering something. "I was watching that show. I was wearing those little wireless headphone ear bud thingies. Yeah! I was listening to the show on those little wireless headphone ear bud thingies – man, what are those things called?"

"Focus, Dad!"

"Right. I was listening to the show with those ... those things because I didn't want to disturb your mom because she was listening to her Christmas carols."

Gunn and Sven turn to Anya. "I love my Carpenters," she offers.

"Mom!" Gunn scolds her.

"But you said, 'That's good, isn't it?' What did you mean by that if you weren't talking about us having a baby?"

"Well, for goodness gracious," Sven exclaims. "I was talking about the show! When the kid with the blanket tells everyone off about the meaning of Christmas. You know that's my favorite part."

"So you didn't hear me tell you ..." Anya asks.

"Do you think I would have forgotten something like that?" Sven says.

Finally, the news hits him.

"We're gonna have a baby?" he asks Anya, putting a hand on her stomach.

"Ayep," she responds.

"Oh, Mama!"

"Oh, Papa!"

Sven leans down and kisses his wife.

Olivia and Tanya stand and push Sven away, as they each take turns congratulating Anya.

"Get back up there, you fool," Anya commands Sven, who returns to his place as his son's best man.

"Is anyone else having a baby?" Pastor Gilnacheck asks loudly from the front of the church.

The crowd laughs as Anya takes her seat, and Gunn and Nathan take their positions once again.

"Shall we continue?" the pastor asks.

Gunn and Nathan nod as they reach out to take each other's hands.

"Right." The pastor continues. "If anyone has just cause —"

Gunn interrupts him. "Let's just skip that part."

But he's too late.

The back door slams open again.

Gunn and Nathan turn their heads and cry out together, "Seriously?!?"

Chapter 27

Standing in the back of the sanctuary is not one person this time, but two people.

The man is soap-opera handsome, with close-cropped dark hair and a stylish suit, and the woman is quite obviously a nun. The outfit gives it away, plus the fact that she crosses herself as soon as she enters the sanctuary.

They both look around the room sheepishly.

The man says to the woman, "I don't think we can slip in unnoticed after all."

"Daniel!" Thomas cries out. He rushes down the aisle and wraps his arms around his on-and-off-again boyfriend, Daniel Van Devere. "You made it!"

"I'm sorry, Thomas," Daniel says. Even his voice sounds like a soap opera star. "I should have been here the whole time."

He looks up at Gunn and Nathan and gives them a quick wave. "Hey, guys!"

They return the wave as Nathan whispers to Gunn, "We really need to start locking doors."

Daniel takes a seat at the back of the sanctuary as Thomas returns to his place beside Gunn.

And then there was one.

"Who's your friend?" Pastor Gilnacheck asks of Daniel.

Daniel glances back at the nun. "No idea. We just showed up at the same time."

"Then who do you belong to, my dear?" the pastor asks politely.

The nun looks around the church in search of someone. Soon everyone is looking around, waiting to see who will stand up to claim her.

Slowly, a figure near the front of the church stands up.

"She's with me."

It's Heather Mancuso.

"Heather! There you are!" the woman cries out as she walks carefully down the aisle to join Heather, who hugs her warmly.

"She's banging a nun?" Anya says to herself, but loud enough for Heather to hear.

"I am not!" Heather hisses. "This is Sister Mary Louisa from the Order of the Sacred Virgin."

Everyone continues to look at Heather, utterly clueless about what she's saying.

"It's over by the mall," Heather offers.

That gets a few nods of recognition from the crowd.

"You see," Heather continues, "I am in love, and I'm getting married."

Everyone waits for the shoe to drop.

"To Jesus Christ."

Silence from the crowd.

Heather looks at Abby, then at Gunn and Nathan, then at Anya, waiting for some kind of reaction.

"Did you hear me? I'm becoming a nun."

There's a long pause before the pastor addresses Gunn and Nathan. "And now we come to a special musical performance from…" He checks his notes. "Abby Mancuso."

Abby makes her way to the front of the church as Heather and Sister Mary Louisa slowly sit down. The disappointment on Heather's face is obvious. On any other day, her announcement would be big news.

Today? Eh, not so much.

* * *

Abby's performance of *Ave Maria* stuns the crowd. Gunn always knew she could sing, but nothing prepared him for this.

Mark and Emma watch proudly, while Heather sobs uncontrollably.

"That's my daughter," she mouths to everyone around her.

When she finished, Abby walks over and gives hugs to both Gunn and Nathan.

"I love you guys," she whispers.

"I know," Gunn responds.

As Abby takes a seat with her family, Pastor Gilnacheck looks solemnly at the two men standing before him.

"Olaf and Nathan have chosen to write their own vows." He checks his notes. "I have been told that they flipped a coin, and that Nathan will go first."

The pastor nods at Nathan, who takes a deep breath before speaking. For the first time today, he looks nervous.

Gunn whispers to Nathan. "Are you ready?"

"Just try to stop me," Nathan replies.

Chapter 28

"I don't know what to say that could top everything that's happened today," Nathan begins, drawing a chuckle from the crowd. "Can we keep this short?" he pleads playfully of Gunn, who nods in agreement.

"I've often wondered what would have happened to me if some random computer hadn't assigned us to be roommates our freshman year. Would we have even met? Would we have ended up here? And the only answer I can come up with is, 'Yes!'"

He reaches out to take Gunn's hands in his own.

"We would have found each other no matter what. That's how strong our love is. It brought us together, it actually taught me how to love, and I believe that it was your love that brought my parents and me closer together."

Martha pulls a lace handkerchief from her purse and delicately dries her eyes as Peter puts an arm around her with a smile.

"We've spent so much time apart – geographically, not emotionally – but it always, somehow, brought us closer together. And now, we're here." Nathan smiles and shakes his head. "Against all the odds, in spite of everyone who tried to keep couples like us apart, we're here. And dontcha know, there's no place I'd rather be.

"I love you, Olaf Gunnunderson, and I'm so ready to be your husband."

Nathan kisses the top of Gunn's hand and stares deep into his eyes.

It's Gunn's turn to take a breath and close his eyes in an attempt to calm his nerves. When he finally opens his eyes, he begins speaking to Nathan as if there was no one else around.

"I was Olaf for the first eighteen years of my life, and then this kid I met at college started calling me 'Gunn.' That was you, by the way."

Nathan nods his head, acknowledging his role in changing Gunn's preferred name.

"I feel like I had a life as Olaf, and don't get me wrong, it was a good life. Parents who loved me, and friends who got me through a lot. But my life as Gunn is better for one reason – because you're in it."

Gunn looks at Nathan's face, and a tear falls from his right eye.

"You gave me the strength to be who I am. You gave me the courage to come out to my parents. You gave me the support I needed to become the man I am. And today, you're giving me the honor of becoming your husband.

"Christmas has always been a special time for my family, and for us, too. And frankly, a lot of people thought we were crazy to have a holiday wedding."

"I did!" Anya cries out with a giggle. That infectious giggle that makes everyone in the church smile and laugh, especially her son and Nathan.

"See, I told you. And yeah, maybe this was a crazy idea. But for me, there's no better way to have a merry little Christmas than to make the yuletide gay with you."

"I love you, Nathan Stanford."

Gunn kisses Nathan's hand.

The rest of the ceremony is a blur for both Gunn and Nathan, as they can barely do anything besides look into each other's eyes with love and anticipation. The pastor talks about the sanctity of marriage, rings are exchanged, and Anya starts crying yet again.

But certain words get the attention of Gunn and Nathan the way nothing else could.

"By the power vested in me by the state of Arizona, I now pronounce you …" The pastor pauses. He knows how to milk the moment for all it's worth. "… husbands for life. You may now each kiss the groom."

All the noise in the church vanishes.

All concerns leave their bodies.

All Gunn and Nathan can see is each other as they lean forward and share their first kiss as a married couple.

They don't see Martha jump to her feet and start clapping her hands, followed by everyone else in attendance.

They don't hear the applause building from the rest of the wedding guests or see the tears of joy on the faces of every single member of the now-joined families.

And they don't see the snow start to fall outside the church – the city's first snowfall in over a hundred years. The local news stations called it "a Christmas miracle." They had no idea how accurate that phrase was. But Gunn and Nathan don't see the snow, not even when it covers the reception tables and hits their three-tiered Christmas-themed wedding cake, topped with two perfect gingerbread men.

What Gunn and Nathan do feel is the love emanating from their friends and families on both sides of the aisle.

Without realizing it, they also feel the love of Gunn's sister, who Anya and Sven will welcome into the world the next year and who will bring so much happiness to the Gunnunderson family.

And they feel the love of the twin boys forming inside Abby who will change their lives completely as they grow up in their beloved house – the house they currently live in, and that Martha and Peter had generously purchased for them as their wedding present.

As the kiss continues, Gunn and Nathan even feel the love of the grandchildren those boys will give them in the future, kids who will watch them grow old and who will be shocked to learn that, one day in their distant past, gay couples weren't allowed to get married.

But most of all, Gunn and Nathan feel the love flowing between them.

In that moment, in that kiss, Gunn realizes that his father was right. On the day of Gunn's birth, Sven whispered in his ear and told him the meaning of life. Today, that statement came true.

Love is all you need.

THE END

About the Author

Rob Williams is an award-winning filmmaker and writer. His movies include *Happiness Adjacent, Shared Rooms, Out To Kill, The Men Next Door, Role/Play, Make The Yuletide Gay, 3-Day Weekend, Back Soon,* and *Long-Term Relationship. Make The Yuletide Gay 2: The Novel* is his second book, following *Make The Yuletide Gay: The Novel.* He lives with his husband, Rodney Johnson, in Palm Springs, California.

Made in the USA
San Bernardino, CA
04 November 2019